YES, YOUR MAJESTY

JENNIFER ANN SHORE

*For Kate, my
lavender girl*

I looped my fingers through the gaps in the chain-link fence.

The last time I stood in this spot, nearly eight months ago, it was to watch humans chase around a soccer ball. Back then, I had to fight my instincts every single second — tearing across the field to sink my teeth in their veins would have been an unexpected and horrifying mid-game experience for everyone — so I gripped the barrier like it was a form of protection.

Now, the metal felt warm beneath my fingertips, and instead of worrying about the accidental slaughter of humans, I was concerned over my schedule. And more accurately, how sluggishly the graduation ceremony progressed forward.

Had I stayed enrolled in high school, following the path of most human teenagers, I'd be sitting next to Eloise, laughing with her to pass the time of the dean's speech, and wearing one of the hideous, overlarge graduation gowns and caps. Instead, I wore one of the many tailored pantsuits Trinity filled my closet with while ignoring the vibrating phone in my pocket.

"Your majesty?"

I closed my eyes in irritation, even though the voice was quiet enough that no human ears could hear how he addressed me.

"Trinity asked me to remind you that to stay on schedule, we should be on our way to the city planning meeting," Jax, one of my bodyguards, said.

He normally didn't get involved in matters of scheduling, usually focusing on standing and observing silently within my vicinity, but Trinity must have grown irritated at my blatant ignoring her. This was the first time since my coronation that I'd done something like that, but I just wanted one little block of time to myself to support a friend and offer my congratulations.

But, as always, duty called.

"Please ask Trinity to call the committee chair and delay the meeting half an hour," I said, turning back to see that the procession finally started. "In return for his scheduling flexibility, I'll fund the next public park project of his choosing."

"Yes, your majesty."

It's not that I had a problem with my two bodyguards, Jax and Wyatt, on a personal level, but I was against the notion of the near-constant security detail in its entirety. It made me feel a little helpless, like I needed to be babysat or was inferior on some level. After all, Uncle Derrick never had to concern himself with frivolous matters like security among humans.

The day after his funeral last December, I sat down with the royals — the two kings and four other queens — and it was one of the many points of discussion. I hadn't expected their concern, and eventually, after outright denying the need for it multiple times, it felt like somewhat of an intervention.

"You need protection," Quinn, the Queen of Cascadia, insisted before accepting a glass of blood from Trinity.

"From what?" I asked her, trying to maintain my composure.

She ignored my question and swirled the glass in her fingertips. "Is this AB-negative?"

"Yes," I answered automatically. "But protection? I can't say I agree with you, Quinn. I'm perfectly capable of protecting myself."

I wanted to remind her I was a queen, just like her, and not a child, but I knew if I spoke the words out loud I would seem incredibly petulant, further proving her point.

While she took a slow sip, I glanced around at the other royals, who were regarding our exchange carefully.

I'd been on the receiving end of that look all my life — by my parents, by the other nobles, hell, by other seniors in high school — and it made me feel like an outsider. And I hated it.

These other royals are supposed to be my equals, and I had to consider that although they were all in on this decision and had some sort of discussion of agreement without me, I'd had the crown on my head for less than a day. By comparison, Isaiah, the King of the Southwest, celebrated the eighty-year anniversary of his coronation last spring.

Maybe they were right.

I could respect it, but that didn't mean I had to like it.

Isabella, the Queen of the Mid-Atlantic, finally spoke up. "We *are concerned for your safety after the explosion at your attempted ritual,"* she drawled.

"It was an accident," I explained. *"The local newspaper in my region confirmed it yesterday."*

"What's the harm in it?" Quinn said, but her growing boredom of this topic became clear in her tone. *"You'll get trustworthy vampires keeping you company and looking out for you, and we will all feel better about it."*

I glanced around the room once again. "And you all feel this way?"

"Even if it's unnecessary, it's in our best interest to ensure your protection," Isaiah assured me.

The collective agreement around me softened the idea, and given the responsibility and plans ahead, I relented.

One of the many things that changed since that discussion — and the rest of the meeting — was that Jax and Wyatt remained within ten feet of me unless we were home at the mansion. Even then, it took a week and a few thousand dollars of security upgrades for them to feel comfortable doing so.

Eloise referred to the pair as "the twins." In the few times I've been able to snag an hour here or there to see her, I could not convince them to go away. I wanted so desperately to be a better and more present friend, but it seemed I was always rushing from one place to the next.

If she didn't have to sleep, it would be much easier.

I tried to get Jax and Wyatt to wait in the car for the duration of the ceremony, but they refused, choosing to hover silently nearby while I watched humans accept their diplomas.

"Eloise Clark," came over the loudspeaker, bringing my

attention back to the makeshift stage in the center of the field.

Claps and hollers erupted from fellow students and the crowd in the stands.

Eloise's mom sat with Charlie's mom, Amy, and his sister, Emma, but they stood on their feet when her name was called, as if that would help project the sound of their cheering better. She waved to them and posed for a picture before heading back to her seat.

If the events of last fall played out differently, I wondered what entourage would be here for me. I assumed that Uncle Derrick and even Trinity would want to come, but I couldn't imagine my parents sitting in the stands, watching me walk across the stage. I'd never completely grasped the hatred my father had for humans — and my very existence — until it was revealed that he conducted horrific experiments on girls, accidentally poisoning and killing his brother in the process.

Instead of a day of celebration with friends and family, I stood on the sidelines. My parents, viewed as betrayers to the crown, were exiled until further notice, and of course, Uncle Derrick died.

The buzzing in my pocket continued, so I finally relented and pulled it out, ignoring the steady stream of names being called out in the ceremony. There were a few missed texts and calls from Trinity, but I couldn't help but smile at Isabella's name.

She and I had grown close over these past few months, fostered because I gave her an iPhone and taught her how to use it. Since then, I've received a regular stream of photos, emojis, and texts throughout the day.

Her nonsensical messages were the only just-for-fun part of the vampire world I experienced, and it was partly because we appreciated humanity in a way that none of the other royals did. She definitely filled a piece of a void I had in Uncle Derrick's absence, and she seemed to enjoy telling me backstories of vampire interactions and talking through various parts of our planning for July First.

As history stands, there's nothing particularly special about that date yet, but it's absolutely going to change the world — July First is the day we vampires will reveal ourselves to humans.

Somewhat naïvely, when I proposed this to my fellow royals, I focused on our regions and our own country, but as we grew further into creating the tenets of a plan for the unveiling, it was clear that this would have a global impact.

We moved quickly but efficiently, coordinating with as many vampire leaders in the world to tell, not ask permission for, what we planned. Nearly every hour of my day was planned out to ensure we'd have a successful, uncomplicated unveiling on July First, but we had a fair amount of struggles along the way.

Working with the human government was taxing, but necessary, as we informed our contacts what was ahead. The senator Uncle Derrick introduced me to last fall came to me directly to voice her support, but she also shared his concern.

"I understand the intention and even its importance, but given today's political climate and the way history hasn't been kind to..." She paused, figuring out the most diplomatic way to say it. "Well, people seem to like white men and no one else."

"Well, we've got plenty of those," I admitted wryly, and she laughed.

I spent the better part of an hour updating her on the latest news, meeting with a few of the human-led companies that were helping us with crisis communication, coordination, research, focus groups, and several other things that turned out to be crucial to our plans.

I came straight to the graduation ceremony from that meeting, immediately standing out in my mint green cropped pantsuit among all the sundresses and polo shirts. I shrugged off the jacket and rolled up the sleeves of the white button-down. It was an attempt to blend in, but somehow I doubted other eighteen-year-olds spent their time wearing blazers and meeting with politicians.

"Charlie Schenley."

Half the crowd cheered for him, and he actually hugged the dean before grabbing his diploma. He stopped for a picture, and Tanner, his friend and fellow teammate, jumped in the frame. The hum of laughter rolled through everyone watching.

When Charlie finally walked back to his seat, his eyes met mine.

He didn't appear entirely surprised to see me, but the joyful expression the camera captured had dissipated. Something harsher took his place, as if he had to toughen his exterior in my presence.

I, on the other hand, soften under his gaze.

I had long ago suppressed our moments together to open up more room in my mind for negotiations, meetings, and planning — but seeing him opened up the floodgate. Hundreds of still images flipped through my mind: Charlie doodling on his notebook in class, the way he smiled while feeding me junk food, how his hand felt in mine, the kiss we shared on the playground.

It all came roaring back to life, as if I had numbed myself into lethargy since I last saw him through the fence on the night of Uncle Derrick's funeral.

"Can I take that for you, your majesty?" Jax asked.

Glad for an excuse to tear my eyes away from Charlie, I nodded at Jax, who happily slung my jacket over his massive forearm.

"Thank you," I said. "Are you enjoying the fresh air?"

"Yes, very much so, thank you."

Occasionally, I played a pathetic game of trying to break Jax and Wyatt from their ultra-rigid personas, but I was never successful. Then again, if someone really wanted to hurt me, it was a good thing they weren't easily distracted.

Still, I found it humorous that Jax and Wyatt had identical skill sets and strengths, given the difference in their appearances. Although Eloise referred to them as "the twins," she specifically gave Jax the nickname "Viking god" because of his size and dirty blond hair.

When Wyatt stood beside me, I could see the top of his head and the uneven spikes of his black hair. He had an overall lightness about him, and I envisioned him as some sort of yoga instructor or life coach before he turned.

"Congratulations to the graduating class," the dean said after all the names had been called.

I looked up from sending a few assorted emojis back to Isabella just in time to see the caps fly in the air. I thought that kind of stuff was just for the movies, but Hollywood seemed to forget the next part of the scene where everyone scrambled to collect their caps in excited panic.

"Mina! You made it." Eloise neglected her fallen cap and ran over, sidestepping the fence to throw her arms around me.

"Of course," I said, returning her embrace, knowing that the twins were eyeing the exchange in irritation. "I couldn't miss it."

Although I made it clear months ago that Eloise was not a threat, they still regarded her carefully. Plus, being in a public setting in this capacity was a rarity for me, and they both seemed to be a little on edge about it.

"Hello, boys," she called, offering them a sly little wave.

Eloise enjoyed trying to break through their seriousness as much as I did.

"Does it ever get boring to be surrounded by such beauty at all times?" Eloise sighed before turning her attention back to me. "Actually, who cares about them? You look like such a damn boss lady!"

I laughed. "Just trying to keep up with you."

She rolled her eyes but still made a show of unzipping the front of her gown to show off a stylish blue dress.

"So you're a high school graduate!" I said excitedly. "With scholarship offers to multiple universities at that. How does it feel?"

"No more exciting than you getting your GED probably," Eloise said, waving her hand in dismissal.

I made time in my packed schedule to go through the motions of becoming an official high school graduate. Even though I technically didn't need to do — it wasn't like I would apply for jobs or college anytime soon — it was something I needed to for me.

"I'm so proud of you!" Eloise's mom, Jan, exclaimed, finally reaching us. "Eloise is the first high school graduate in the family. Did you know that, Mina?"

"That's fantastic," I said, ignoring Eloise's eye roll. "How are you celebrating?"

Jan rubbed her hands together in excitement. "We're all going out to dinner tonight to that new sushi restaurant. You should come with us!"

Her mother was overly enthused by our friendship. I wondered if that would change after July First or if she would be an advocate for vampires and myself.

"Mina is busy running her empire, Mom," Eloise said, deflecting for me.

"On a Saturday?" Jan asked. "Surely whatever it is can wait until Monday. We're celebrating, after all!"

"The business doesn't have nights and weekends off," I said, feeling my phone buzz. "I'm running late now for a city planning meeting, unfortunately."

"That's a lot of responsibility for a teenager," Jan said, slightly awed.

Uncle Derrick made being the King look easy, mostly because he didn't have to justify the never-ending work ethic of vampires to humans who needed things like mental breaks and extended periods of rest.

I shrugged. "I'm not your typical teenager, I suppose. Your siblings aren't here, Eloise?"

"They didn't want to sit through the ceremony, so we're swinging by the house and picking them up later," Eloise said. "Not everyone can be as dedicated to their older sibling as this one." Eloise gestured to Emma, who bounced in Charlie's arms as they approached.

"Eloise! Mina! Hi!" Emma screeched, wiggling in excitement.

"Hello, Emma Rose Schenley," I said with a smile. "And, Charlie, hi. Congratulations!"

"Thanks," Charlie said the word to me, but his eyes landed on Jax and Wyatt.

I stood awkwardly in his presence, offering no explanation as to why the two vampires were standing behind me.

Just as I turned to make conversation with Charlie, Jax stepped forward. "My apologies for the interruption, but we have another appointment downtown," he said.

Frankly, I wasn't even annoyed at the reminder; I was just glad he remembered not to address me as "your majesty."

"Are you sure you can't join us?" Jan asked me one more time.

I offered her a sad smile and shake of my head. "Sleepover soon, though, Eloise?"

My question was met with an enthusiastic nod and another limb-entangling hug that I really didn't want to break free from.

2

It took me longer than I wanted to get into the groove of being the Queen of Appalachia.

I embodied the pinnacle of regality as best I could, but meeting with humans, vampires, royals, nobles, politicians, and CEOs almost every hour of the day drained me, and I took in double the amount of blood I considered normal.

Trinity kept me on track, staying by my side physically or connected through the phone and the twins. I understood more than ever why Uncle Derrick wholeheartedly trusted her.

Frankly, I'd be lost without her, and I tried to give her a new, fancier title and pay raise once a week, but she refused and claimed if I didn't stop trying, she'd start working for free or put money toward politicians whom I hated. Given that she had as much access to the businesses, finances, and accounts as I did, I took her threat seriously and backed off.

Those who worked close to Uncle Derrick, and now

myself, didn't have much of a personal life to indulge, anyway. It wasn't that vampires lived frugally — in fact, most I knew lived in luxury, but there seemed to be an innate purpose in the way they own and do things, whereas humans want to appear more wealthy than they really are.

Humans work long hours and years on end, living for the weekends and weeks of vacation. They like to justify giving themselves a break, figuring out the balance between work and life, but if there's one thing vampires are better at, it's simply existing.

I have to think it's because vampires have the gift of time. Not sleeping, or even getting tired, opens up so much more time, as well as the longer lifespans — the only exceptions to this being the rumored three-hundred-year-old vampire hiding in London and those of us half-human, half-vampires.

We're the exceptions to the norm in vampire culture, and I've happily found my place with a foot in each world, trying to pull the best from each. I wish everyone else saw it that way, embracing the differences and unknowns, but it wasn't. The twins were a consequence of my perceived weakness.

One of the many things Uncle Derrick made me promise before he died was that I would never allow myself to feel inferior to other vampires.

"Brute strength and speed should not overpower your voice, Mina," Uncle Derrick told me while hovering a few inches off the ground — just because he could.

In the last month of his life, his energy was nearly bursting out of his body. It was both amusing and irritating that he flew more often than he would be on the ground. I cut him some slack, though, because it was a harmless reprieve between bouts of coughing up liters of blood.

"Your majesty," Philip said, pulling my attention toward him. "The other region representatives and I have come up with a plan on expanding the distribution network, as we discussed the last time we met."

He picked up where my father left off after I banished him from the region in January.

Unfortunately, my father's role in accidentally poisoning and killing Uncle Derrick didn't outright violate anything in the Code of Conduct, so there wasn't much I could do under vampire rules other than change his physical location. I promised myself that one day soon, I would do right by those girls he harmed, but for now, I had to keep pressing on.

I spoke to the issue at length with the other royals, and the best solution we could see fit was to put his skills to use elsewhere, in a less-than-ideal situation. Isabella volunteered to have him in her region as a favor to me, and last I checked, he was stuck indoors most of the time with mind-numbing paperwork.

I couldn't help the frown on my face, but I pulled it back into my standard neutral expression when I caught Theo's gaze. Locking eyes with him always made me feel at ease, even more so when he offered me a tight smile.

"Do you need me to review it here?" Philip asked me.

"Trinity shared your presentation, and I agree with the plan in its entirety," I told him. "Commendable work."

I wasn't lying; he was doing a superb job leading the charge. It was amazing how quickly people could work toward a common goal, and assuring the viability of our blood distribution was crucial to the unveiling.

"Thank you, your majesty."

"Is there anything stopping it from moving forward?"

"We have run into some difficulty with a few of the regions in Canada."

"Oh?" I asked.

"They're pushing back because of the healthcare complications in our country at the moment."

I sighed, getting flashbacks to the Health project in human school last fall. "I understand their reservations," I admitted. "I'll see what I can do to clear some red tape for you."

From what I recalled, Quinn, the Queen of Cascadia, had a fantastic rapport with all the royals up north. "Trinity, can you make a note of it?"

She nodded, not looking up from her tablet. No doubt she was already firing off an email to coordinate several meetings to fulfill my promise.

"Anything else I can help with?" I asked Philip, and when he declined, I turned to the rest of the nobles around the table. "Nothing else that needs to be brought up while we're all together?"

I got no response.

"Thank you all for attending this month's meeting and for bearing with my updates on the unveiling," I said, making eye contact with each vampire in the room as I spoke, another tip from Uncle Derrick. "It appears we are all set up for success, and it wouldn't be possible without the guidance and input from every one of you. Please reach out to myself and Trinity if you need to discuss anything further."

I acknowledged the collective bows of the nobles before they followed Trinity out, leaving Theo and me alone.

When the door closed, he stood up from his position at the end of the table and collapsed in the chair beside me. Theo's staying back for us to debrief and vent about the monthly sessions with the nobles had become a recent routine for us, and I made sure that Trinity blocked a few extra minutes on my schedule for these few precious moments with him.

Unofficially, Theo was my right-hand man in the nobles, and they all regarded him as such. It was pure nepotism, but this was a monarchy, not a democracy, and I needed someone I could trust.

"That went well," Theo said.

I removed my crown, placing it on the table in front of me, and fluffed my hair. Every single time I laid eyes on the red rubies, I thought of Uncle Derrick, wishing he could see me wear it. There wasn't a day that went by that I didn't wish he was still here to guide me.

"I think so, too," I agreed. "But I think there's an under-lying tone of nervousness with the unveiling. I'm not sure how many of them will ultimately come forward on July First."

One of the most contentious parts of what we royals eventually agreed to was that we wouldn't force anyone to reveal their natures to humans. We and the others around the globe agreed to out ourselves as vampires, but we put no pressure on the others to do so.

As much preparation as we put into this, we ultimately

weren't sure what the reaction from the general population of humans would be, and we wouldn't force anyone to take that risk.

Human governments kept tabs on their populations by identification, social security numbers, and whatever secret spying they were doing on citizens. Given that all vampires were once human, they could integrate and thrive in human society if they wished without complications. Vampires could continue as normal without outing themselves as long as they followed our Code of Conduct and lived within the rules that the human governments set forth.

The blood distribution network was a crucial part of our unveiling because it staved off what we all assumed would be a major concern for humans. We expected some would feel they were just walking, vulnerable blood bags. Of course, we were certain there were going to be other, unpredictable complications, and we'd have to work with those as they came to fruition.

"I know you've been incredibly busy since your coronation. Actually 'busy' is probably an understatement, considering you've been booked twenty-four hours a day dealing with humans and vampires across time zones…" He trailed off in a way that made me think I would not enjoy whatever he had to say next. "But Eva asked me to speak with you."

I wasn't exactly the most hospitable guest the last time Evaline, Theo's aunt and one badass witch, was in my presence.

It was after I found out the atrocities my father had committed, and I refused blood to the point that I was nearly catatonic. Theo begged her to come by, knowing how terrified she was to be without the protection in her own residence, but she did, ultimately declaring there was nothing she could do to help.

Since then, whether by choice or by happenstance, she kept her distance. I had enough challenges at the moment with vampires and humans that other mythic humanoids were not a priority.

"How is she doing?" I asked him.

He might be the only vampire in existence with a trusted relationship with witches. Their blood relation helped, as did the fact that he kept some of his power after he turned. I haven't pried too much into his abilities, just like he respected my own privacy with my more human traits.

"She's good," Theo blurted, dampening my concern.

My phone buzzed on the tabletop, and the sound drew both our gazes.

Charlie.

Until last weekend, contact and all Charlie-related thoughts did not exist, but maybe he had the same rush of memories and feelings as I did and wanted some closure. I reached forward and declined his call, definitely not wanting to have that conversation or whatever else he wanted to discuss in front of Theo.

"Why does it say 'husband' on your phone?" Theo asked lightly. "Did a marriage happen I wasn't aware of? Hopefully, an arranged one?"

It felt like it was in another lifetime that Charlie swiped my phone from me in Health and entered that name.

"It was just a joke," I said with a tone of finality I hoped would stop Theo from asking questions.

I hardly recognized the version of myself whose days were spent concentrating on making Charlie blush and pretending to learn in high school classrooms. Now, I barely had free time to myself, let alone the opportunity to spend my time thinking about an adolescent human and indulging in a frivolous romance.

And if I did...

Being in Theo's presence was like having a weight lifted off my chest, like I could fully relax and not maintain the front I had to hold up in front of everyone else. My gaze dropped to his hands, recalling the way he once held me in a moment of passion. I had to force down the feelings and blink away *those* thoughts.

Although I'm a teenage royal, I'm definitely not a saint.

I forced all the air out of my lungs, telling my body to recalibrate to the present.

"What did Eva want?" I asked him.

Theo shifted forward, putting his elbows on the table. "You remember how she deals in favors, not in monetary payment?"

I nodded. "Of course."

We owed Eva because she agreed to participate in a vampire ritual last fall. My vampire great-grandmother had bribed a witch in her time to keep the first King of Appalachia's blood viable before he turned, and it was eventually turned into a key part of a ritual performed to all of the heirs of the "bloodline" for continuity's sake.

Although the ritual never happened because of the explosion — and then my insistence that it should be removed from the Code of Conduct — we were still in her debt. I didn't mind, honestly. I would be happy to help her because of her relation to Theo alone, but she also created a potion to ease Uncle Derrick's symptoms as he was dying. For that, I would forever be grateful.

"She is asking for the protection that King Derrick promised her," Theo said.

"Now?" I asked.

He nodded, knowing how horrible the timing of this was.

"Is she having trouble with the werewolves?"

Theo merely shrugged. "Better to let her explain."

I hated how cryptic that response was. "Well, if it's not urgent enough for you to tell me now, I'll have Trinity set up a meeting after the unveiling."

"Fair enough," he agreed. "I'll give Eva the heads up."

As if on cue, Trinity popped in. "Jax and Wyatt are waiting for you in the car," she said. "Board meeting for the plastics manufacturing company."

"Right," I said, standing up to follow her.

"Thank you, your majesty," Theo said, bow and tone were totally sincere.

I turned back to him, realizing my own rudeness.

He wasn't some mayor or sales vice president at one of my companies. This was Theo — the one who has challenged me and stood by me since I first met him at my parents' house — and he was being too polite, treating me just like everyone else.

That jolted me to a stop.

He waved me off before I could open my mouth. "I understand."

I couldn't afford to alienate him, and more importantly, I couldn't bear it.

Without hesitation, I threw my arms around him, and he responded immediately, sliding his hands around my waist. It felt just like I remembered, but somehow, I appreciated it more in this moment. This felt like an indulgence, not a reaction to the words he told me in the rain.

"I'm so sorry." I inhaled, taking in the mixture of metal, lavender, and sage on his skin before I pulled back.

"Why are you apologizing?"

"I just wish we had more time together."

The side of his mouth quirked up into a smile. "I miss you, too, Mina."

I reached for his hand and squeezed it reassuringly before I went off, crown gripped between my fingers, and on with the endless days.

3

I eventually called Charlie back.

Our conversation was rushed and between meetings, and he was acting a little coy, saying that he was just thinking of me and was hoping to catch up in person. It would be nice to see and talk to him after all this time, but selfishly, I wanted our reunion to be dual purpose — finally telling him the truth that he already suspected and revealing my vampirism to Eloise.

And that's how on the last day of June, Charlie finally came through the gates to my home, truck roaring up the driveway.

Technically, I would break the Code and the rules I set out for my own region. We had iron-clad contracts and embargoes in place for the July First deadline, but it didn't stop me.

I justified it to myself one million different ways, and then gave up, deciding that one of the few privileges I could claim for myself would be to tell two people I could trust.

Besides, they would probably stay until after midnight, anyway.

When vampires, nobles, and business associates arrive, Trinity usually greets them with well-practiced formality. But in this case, I wanted to let them in myself. I begged Trinity and the twins to make themselves scarce for the evening, not needing their vampire hearing to listen in on what might be a very personal conversation.

"Welcome back," I said to Eloise, opening the door before she had time to knock.

She squealed in excitement. "I can't believe I haven't seen you since graduation!"

"I know."

"Are the twins here?" she asked, whipping her head around as if she expected them to be lurking — which, in all fairness, they would be if we were outside my house.

I shook my head. "They have the night off."

"Bummer," she sighed, stepping into the foyer. "Guess I'll just have to settle for you."

"Nice to get through the gates this time," Charlie said with a full grin.

"I am sorry about that, you know."

We stood for a beat, facing each other, until he moved in for a hug. I accepted the embrace, which seemed like an adequate, friendly greeting, but I stayed rigid, holding my breath until he released me.

"This is a really nice place," Charlie breathed, taking in the house's interior.

I once had grand ideas about taking my time to enjoy the process of filling my house with furniture, to make it more enticing for humans, but with how busy Trinity and I have been, she found a fantastic interior designer who took care of it all for us.

As an endless line of trucks and movers brought furniture and decor into the house, it became clear that my personal utilitarian style was not what we needed. I thought my bedroom was sufficient with the vanity table and lone couch in front of the fire, but the designer coordinated the large, soft printed rug with the wall decor and throw pillows.

Beds were added to each bedroom, and some spaces were dedicated to other uses, like a workout space and a meditation room. I never spent time in either, but I supposed as I eventually wanted to host more human guests, they were nice to have.

As we made our way up to the library, I tried to see everything from Charlie's eyes.

My home was too large for a single teenager, but I took pride in it because Uncle Derrick lived here and appreciated the space, and just being here made me feel closer to him.

"So your uncle just left everything to you?" Charlie asked. "And your parents took off after the funeral?"

"Yes, and yes." I was going to reveal a lot of truths tonight, and all of those details didn't necessarily need to be part of it.

I kept most of the books Uncle Derrick had on the shelves that lined the walls. The intimidating wingback chairs had been replaced with three large leather sofas, organized in a U shape in front of the fire. A brand new television hung above the mantle, which Charlie stared at more closely than anything else.

The chess board, where Uncle Derrick and I played

dozens of matches, had been relocated to my office, and I stared at it longingly from time to time.

"Make yourselves comfortable," I encouraged, waving to the plates of food that Trinity had a chef arrange for them.

"Is this a charcuterie plate?" Eloise asked tentatively, eyeing the spread.

I hesitated until my memory jogged, flipping back to the party we all attended last fall where Tanner surprised us with his food knowledge. Eloise and Charlie laughed at his expense.

"Have you two spoken since graduation?" I asked Eloise.

Eloise and Tanner had one of those roller coaster relationships where they spent more time chasing each other and arguing than anything else. It seemed utterly exhausting to me, and I only had to experience it second-hand in text messages and phone calls when Eloise updated me.

She wrinkled her nose. "No, and it's probably better that way."

"You always say that," Charlie accused, popping a grape into his mouth. "And then a week later you're all over each other again."

"Shut up, Charlie."

I've missed banter and conversations that didn't involve blood, politics, and all the other seriousness I was dealing with.

But I was about to merge the two worlds, and suddenly, I felt a little uneasy.

"Do you two want something to drink?" I asked, opening a can of Sprite for myself.

They both shook their heads and watched me take a small sip.

I wanted to do something normal and human before I changed the dynamic between us forever.

Dragging it out would only make me feel worse, so I went for it. "I wanted to tell you something," I started. "Something huge."

I took another sip and placed the can on the table.

"Are you two back together and didn't tell me?" Eloise demanded, her gaze snapping between the two of us. "Because if neither one of you—"

"No," Charlie answered for me. "We aren't."

I rubbed my hands on my jeans, trying to stop myself from fidgeting. I regularly faced off with old white men in suits, but somehow, this seemed like a daunting task.

Eloise took in my expression. "What's wrong?"

I tried to smile. "I'm ready to have that conversation now, Charlie, just like I promised."

His mouth dropped open in surprise, but he closed it and sat up, preparing himself to hear me out and hopefully help me deal with Eloise's reaction.

"It's..." I stopped. "Well, you see, Eloise..." I had months to prepare for this, and I was embarrassed that I struggled to find the words.

"Mina's a vampire," Charlie said, as if it were the most casual thing in the world.

Vampire.

The word I wouldn't let him say out loud all those months ago was now in the open.

I pictured telling Eloise hundreds of times with all ranges of emotion coming from her. I thought of the worst scenario, which was her being disgusted by my existence, then storming off to join some sort of anti-vampire group that would undoubtedly form after July First. I also imagined her happy, after some disbelief at first, not caring in the slightest that I drank blood and spent most of the day wearing a crown.

The one reaction I hadn't expected from her was laughter, and it was the one I got.

"Not you, too, Charlie," she said, like his words were some big practical joke. "Even Brooklyn dropped that act once Mina quit showing up to school."

Charlie offered me an "I tried" look.

I sighed. I needed to pull myself together and make her understand.

I closed my eyes, mentally willing the stuttering and unease to leave my body. I pictured myself wearing my crown and the black ball gown I wore to Uncle Derrick's funeral and my coronation. It was the most confident I had ever felt in my existence, and I needed that now.

I had to explain it to Eloise, to make her understand I wasn't a threat, that I was the same Mina she's always known, but that we had a difference in diet, speed, and sleeping habits.

If I couldn't convince her to be okay with who I was, how the hell would I be able to get everyone else in the region, country, and world to accept our existence?

"Charlie's telling the truth," I said slowly.

Her laughter fizzled out, and her gaze flicked between the two of us. "Is this a joke? You're trying to get me to believe that you're a vampire."

I shook my head. "Well, technically I'm only half-vampire," I explained. "My father and mother were together when she was still human. It's actually somewhat of a miracle that I was born because in the few recorded cases of half-human, half-vampires, most of the babies kill their mothers before their birth."

Which is why my father conducted those awful experiments last fall, trying to impregnate girls and eventually turn the children into vampires. I pushed that aside for now, but I had hopes and plans for a reckoning for that.

Eloise stayed perfectly still, but her eyes followed my hands as they moved, so I continued. "Most vampires are turned, not born, so I'm somewhat of an outcast. I've always felt a pull toward my human side, which is why I begged my uncle to let me go to high school last year. I wanted to learn more about humans and to integrate into that society."

"To integrate into that society," Eloise repeated.

"To make friends and experience—"

"I know what the phrase means, Mina." There was an edge to her voice I hadn't heard since we left the disastrous sleepover with Brooklyn, and I hated that it was directed toward me.

Eloise stood up, needing to pace while she processed this. "And you knew?" she asked Charlie.

"I figured it out," Charlie admitted. "Everything added up over time, but I wasn't sure until I broke into her house before Homecoming and found about fifty blood bags in her refrigerator."

"You drink blood?" Recognition hit her. "Your weird diet," she added, piecing it together.

I took another sip of Sprite, just to show her I could. "I

can eat human food because I'm partially alive. All of my organs work, although they're mostly just decoration at this point. If a normal vampire ate or drank anything, they'd probably just have to hold it in their throats until they could spit it back out later. Or it would just decay inside them, which doesn't seem very pleasant at all."

Eloise considered this for a minute, and I watched her for any reaction or emotion that told me she was okay with this. Or at the very least, that she accepted I was telling the truth.

She crossed the room with unusual quickness for a human, not stopping until her shins hit my knees.

"Prove it," Eloise said, her tone challenging.

"What?" I balked.

She held up her wrist, taunting me by waving it in front of my face. "Prove that you're a vampire. Drink my blood."

"Eloise," Charlie warned.

I stood up and gently pushed her away from me back toward Charlie. "You don't want that," I promised.

Eloise started laughing again. "See? I feel like you two are just messing with me."

Some humans are visual learners, others need textbooks and explanations, but I cast all of that aside for the moment because what Eloise needed more than anything at this moment was indisputable truth.

She needed to see what I was before she'd accept it. If I drank from a blood bag, she could argue it as fake, but if I attempted to drink from her wrist, I might kill her.

I closed my eyes, knowing that she was watching my every moment, and I gave into my vampire instincts. Not enough where I was out of control and couldn't stop myself, but I attuned myself to their heartbeats, the blood pumping through their veins, the delicateness of their skin...

When I opened my eyes again, I felt positively feral.

I parted my lips to reveal the sharpness of my fangs. I sprang over the back of the couch with ease, showing off my speed slightly, before I pushed it, zooming around the room in circles. I did a dozen laps around them in ten seconds.

It was exhilarating to finally be my true self around them, like I was shedding the reserved and polite version of myself.

After tomorrow, there was no need to play down my speed or my strength, and the realization spurred me further.

I hit the side of one of the vacant couches with my palm, and it shot across the room. I sprinted and jumped, landing swiftly on the cushions with a grin on my face. I wanted to jump up and hang from the chandelier, but I wasn't sure it could hold my weight.

This was freedom, I realized, and I wanted all vampires to have it.

"Holy shit," Eloise breathed.

Seeing her shaking hands in my peripheral vision righted me.

My smile faded when I took in their ashen faces — Charlie looked slightly terrified, and Eloise seemed fairly impressed.

I forced a set of breaths from my lungs and tried to return to normal, driving my fangs back into my gums. I slid the furniture in place, using it as a barrier between us while I waited for their reaction.

It was Charlie who spoke first. "Why are you telling us this?" His voice was quiet but strong.

"I've wanted to tell you for a long time, Charlie, you know that," I reminded him. "And I wanted to make sure you heard it from me."

His eyebrows pulled together. "No, I mean, why are you telling us this *now*? After all this time? I mean, whenever I tried to say the word 'vampire' in the past, you looked as though you were in severe pain and cut me off."

"Tomorrow, July First, there is going to be an unveiling of vampires to humans."

It took me two hours to dive deep into all the planning and details.

I filled in the gaps about my abilities, how I differed from vampires, and explained how the regions worked. The only response I got from either of them was a follow-up question or a nod, which wasn't exactly reassuring.

"Are all vampires this rich?" Eloise asked, gesturing to her surroundings.

I paused. "Well, that's another thing, my Uncle Derrick was the King of Appalachia, and when he died, everything passed on to me."

"That explains the crown I saw the day of his funeral," Charlie said as more dots connected in his mind. "The day of his funeral. That's why you wouldn't let me in. All the vampires were here."

I nodded. "I couldn't guarantee your safety, and frankly, it was better for both of us to spend time apart."

"Wait a second, you're telling me you're a freaking QUEEN?" Eloise shrieked.

Out of everything I told her after my demonstration, this seemed to throw her off the most.

"You, who got bullied in high school by some mean-spirited wench, are the Queen of the Vampires?"

From anyone else, this statement would seem off-putting and venomous, like how could some lowly high school loser be something of high value in another life? But from Eloise, it seemed hilarious, like she couldn't handle the contrast between the two worlds.

"Well, not of all the vampires, just of the ones in this region," I said. "Although, typically if it's known that I'm a queen, regardless of location, I'm bowed to. In fact, even some human politicians I've met have followed our proto-col, but I prefer not to wear the crown all day. Honestly, it's cumbersome."

Eloise laid back on the couch, putting her feet up on the arm as if this was too much to bear. "My best friend is a freaking goddess queen!"

"I'm still your best friend, then?" I asked, trying to not sound too absolutely pathetic about it.

She looked at me like I was insane for insinuating that wasn't the case.

"As if you could get rid of me that easily. It's not like you can do magic or turn at the full moon." She stopped herself and sat up. "Wait, are vampires the only beings I need to know about?"

4

After another hour of questions, Trinity brought up another round of food for them and a mug of blood for me.

I think she was glad to see the conversation going so well, even smirking when Eloise's morbid curiosity over my blood preferences came about. I happily obliged her, but it felt somewhat strange to be completely open and honest with her, like it was too good to be true.

There was no shame in being a half-human, half-vampire queen. It's not like it was my choice, but I was grateful for the support.

Eloise turned on the television, joking about trying to find some reruns of *The Vampire Diaries* for us to watch together. I explained to her about how Charlie tried to use television and movies to get answers from me while he fell asleep in a fort. Charlie got me back by telling Eloise about the junk food rankings and how hilarious my reaction was the first time I tried pop.

A knock sounded at the front door, and I perked up, curious who was visiting unannounced.

"What is it?" Eloise asked, stifling a yawn.

"Someone's at the door," I said.

Charlie eyed me. "How do you know?"

"Advanced hearing," Eloise explained, as if she were now the foremost expert on vampirism.

I inhaled deeply and relaxed.

"You can *smell* people, can't you?" Eloise asked.

"Yes."

"What do I smell like?"

"Do you really want to know?"

She nodded. "Yes!"

I sniffed. "Coconuts. Vanilla. Maple syrup. And, um, Cheetos."

Charlie laughed, snatching the bag from her hands.

"Well, I suppose it could be worse," Eloise said, wrestling the bag back. "I mean, Mina *has* been in your presence after soccer practice, Charlie, and she still tolerates you."

"Hey, Mina, I thought we—" The smile on Theo's face faltered when he took in the relaxed position of the three of us.

"Theo!" Eloise said excitedly. "I didn't know you'd be here."

He dropped the bag of blood and two champagne flutes on one of the side tables. "I could say the same thing," he said lightly, accepting her embrace. "It's good to see you again. I hear you're a high school graduate now?"

Eloise beamed. "Both Charlie and I are headed off to college in the fall to CMU."

"Great school," he complimented before turning his attention to the blond-haired human eyeing him from the couch. "And you must be Charlie?"

He jumped up, smoothing his hair back off his forehead.

My mind spun at watching the two of them react. I was helpless but deadly curious, choosing to see it unfold in front of me.

Charlie extended his hand, and Theo shook it.

"Ah," Charlie yelped. "You're a vampire, too?"

Theo looked at me with surprise.

I shrugged. "It's going to come out in a few hours, anyway."

"And you're the human boyfriend?" Theo asked Charlie, but his eyes didn't leave mine.

Charlie awkwardly laughed as a response, and thankfully, Eloise pivoted the conversation.

"Theo, where have you been lately?" she said. "You're never around when I am. I look for you every single time I'm in the Strip District."

"You two have met?" Charlie asked.

There were so many questions and answers happening here that the worlds colliding finally became too much. Weeks of back-to-back meetings didn't faze me, but all this personal emotion was becoming my undoing.

Thankfully, Trinity saved me by knocking on the door frame. This woman has made a career of interrupting at the right time. I should definitely try to give her another raise.

"Your majesty," she said with uncharacteristically wide eyes. "You're needed immediately."

I honestly couldn't tell if it was an act to get me out of the situation or if something was legitimately wrong.

"What is it, Trinity?" I asked her.

She glanced around the room.

"It's fine," I reassured her. "You can speak freely."

"A few media outlets broke our embargo," she said, grabbing the remote and flipping to a news channel.

Sure enough, the "BREAKING NEWS" ticker on the bottom revealed the truth of our existence, and the anchors were in deep discussion about it, showing clips from various films and movies to sensationalize the coverage.

I groaned.

We had specifically put a deadline in place that made sense for publications in various time zones. Not that it was entirely surprising. It was the biggest story of the year — or maybe the biggest story of all time.

"And once a few started, the rest went right along with it," Trinity explained with a grimace. "You're needed in your office to join in on a conference call. The other royals are dialing in now."

"Right," I told her before I turned to Charlie and Eloise. "I'm really sorry about this. I know it's cutting our night short, but Trinity can escort you—"

"Night cut short?" Eloise jumped in. "It's just getting started. I'm not abandoning you like this. Plus, I want to see what the other kings and queens look like."

I looked to Theo for his thoughts, but he merely shrugged. "I suppose there's no harm in it," he said.

They all followed me down to my office. It was normally tidy, but over the past few weeks, it became organized chaos. The closest comparison I could make to human terms was that the walls looked like a presidential election night, with maps drawn and polls with predictions on how regions would respond to the news.

I sat behind my desk, and Trinity patched me into the video conference.

From where I sat, the other royals were projected on the gigantic screen, but they couldn't see the humans and vampires who were sitting to my right.

"Where's Isabella?" I asked, noting her absence.

"She's going to be on CNN shortly," Isaiah explained. "They agreed to a last-minute emergency broadcast, even though it's way past prime time now."

Trinity gestured to the muted television screen to my left where Isabella looked composed, beautiful, and every bit a queen as she patiently waited for her turn to speak. I pulled out my phone, sending her a text telling her those things even though I knew she wouldn't be able to check it until she was off camera.

The other royals were in problem-solving mode, multi-tasking and updating all of us on what they were hearing from their region and friends abroad while figuring out how to change our plans.

Isaiah had decades of experience in the human corporate world before he turned and became the king of his region. His advice and input had been valuable for all of us, and he helped wrangle the best of the human businesses to help us.

Ultimately, we agreed to focus on our individual regions, making damage control more manageable instead of the big national and global splash. We'd have check-ins every few hours and send updates through our secretaries to keep track of all the news coverage.

As the other vampire royals continued on, I asked Trinity for the research she had pulled on the biggest newspapers and news sites in the region, along with all their numbers on social media followings and reach. In a flash, she retrieved it from her office and slid it in front of me. I went through the list, circling the publications I wanted to try to speak with tomorrow.

"Mina, when I spoke with the head of the crisis communication firm before I joined the call, they reiterated the importance of leaning into your human side," Isaiah said. "Relatability is our greatest asset at this point."

"Sure," I said confidently. "I can do that."

They moved on to the next topic, and I couldn't help but smirk. So many vampires saw humanity as a weakness, and now, it was one of our greatest strengths.

When the call finally ended, I apologized to Charlie and Eloise profusely, but they waved me off.

"It was kind of interesting to see," Charlie admitted. "But I think Eloise is still in shock."

"Well, it's not every day that your world turns upside down, Charlie. I think I'm doing relatively well considering you've had *months* to process this, and I've had a few hours."

I laughed and relaxed back into my chair.

"Mina, the nobles are asking for an update," Theo said, holding up his phone that was buzzing with notifications. "I'll take care of that while you finish up here."

"Thank you," I said to his back.

He answered the phone and walked out of the room, with Eloise's eyes glued to him.

Charlie yawned. "Well, I guess it's time for us humans to head home."

I glanced at the sheet in front of me. "Charlie, do you think I could speak to you for a minute?" I asked him, tapping on the paper.

Eloise gave me a quick hug goodbye before Trinity led her out, leaving Charlie and me alone.

I leaned against the front of my desk, trying to appear casual instead of antsy at asking for a favor.

He looked at me expectantly, and for the first time tonight, and in months, I gave him my full attention.

"Do you think your father would do an interview with me?" I asked.

Charlie blinked, expecting me to tackle a different topic now that it was just us — I dreaded that discussion just as much as I did willingly spending time with his father.

But I pressed on. "His paper has an incredible presence online. He wasn't completely wrong when he threatened me with the exposé on my uncle last fall. He has a big voice, and it would really mean a lot to me if he would agree to it."

"Of course he will," Charlie said, full of confidence.

I crossed my arms on my chest. "You're that certain?"

He bobbed his head for a second. "Well, you might have to agree to be on video and do other promotion stuff, but this is such a big story, I bet he'd jump at the opportunity."

I laughed. "You're right."

"I know," he said.

"And, Charlie, I'm glad I finally got to tell you everything," I admitted. "It feels good to clear the air."

At that, he stood up, bridging the distance between us.

He moved with the same swift deliberateness and purpose that I recognized from when he drilled the soccer ball twenty yards across the field to set up for a shot on goal.

"I understand, Mina. I really do. Last fall, when you cut me out so suddenly, it hurt like hell. Still, some part of me knew it was just temporary, and that's why I didn't put up too much of a fight." His expression turned to something more determined. "Do you think with everything out in the open we can have another chance?"

I forced a cool exterior, but internally I scrambled for a way to back out of this.

Charlie fell deeply for me, I knew this, because I reciprocated his feelings to some degree. But it was different.

I went into our relationship knowing it wouldn't last, but I blindsided him. I hurt him when I pushed him away. I hated myself for it — but Charlie was too perfect, too human to get involved in the affairs of vampires.

"I don't think so, Charlie," I told him.

He nodded, not totally surprised. "We could have made it work," he said.

I couldn't decide if he said those words for himself or for me, but I didn't agree with him at all.

As nice as it was to envision myself in a normal, wonderfully human life, I couldn't imagine Charlie in the vampire one. It was going to be a long fight for equality for vampires, and to ask him to give up everything to join in the cause... it wasn't fair for me to ask him to do that.

It wouldn't be impossible to do it, but to change the entire course of his life based on teenage emotions — especially volatile, hormone-driven teenage boy ones — was not something I was willing to do.

It was partly my fault, I know, for pushing him away and treating him like he was made of glass, but I needed to be direct and clear. He didn't need to be hopeful, for both our sakes.

"I wasn't, and am not, willing to, Charlie," I said as kindly as I could. "I love that you've embraced all of this and liked me for who I am, but you don't know what you would be signing up for or the danger you'd be putting yourself in. I care about you so deeply, and a part of me will always feel that way, but feeling that way meant I had to get over my romantic feelings toward you, as wonderful as they were, because I can't give you everything."

Charlie ground his teeth as I spoke, letting the words roll over him.

"It's not because I'm not trying hard enough. In fact, trying not to fall in love with you took an incredible amount of energy that I can't bear to go through again," I admitted.

His life was complicated enough with his own family dynamics, and I would never ask him to take on an entire unknown world and the responsibility with it. I knew that should be his choice to make. I couldn't live with myself if I pulled him into this madness with me.

It was probably the most selfish thing I could do, but my conscience was clear.

I gripped the edge of the desk, waiting for him to meet my gaze once again.

He swallowed and nodded, accepting my words. "Friends then?"

"I'd like that," I admitted.

I wrapped my arms around his neck, pulling him down to me. He obliged my embrace, sliding his hands along my back and pressing me more firmly against him into the scent of spearmint and grass.

The sound of crunching wood caught my attention, and when we broke apart, I saw Theo trying to nonchalantly discard the broken bits of the door frame.

Charlie breathed heavily beside me, as if I had stolen all the air from his lungs, but he didn't back away from me.

I knew how this looked from Theo's eyes, but I didn't have time to explain the compromising position because the next words out of his mouth were like a knife to the stomach.

"There is rioting in every major city, and many groups are already forming to hunt and kill vampires."

He paused, flicking his gaze between Charlie and me once more.

"The humans are turning against us," he said, but I didn't think that was the only reason he sounded absolutely gutted.

5

Daniel Schenley greeted me warmly.

His enthusiasm was obvious in his expression and his handshake, and I tried to return it.

Apparently, time can heal all wounds, or at least, it can make a human forget about how the last time we spoke, he was vaguely threatening me.

Maybe he just he hated my uncle for being rich and unavailable, and now that the truth was out about vampirism, he found some level of understanding for the aloofness — or he was hungry enough for the story that he didn't care either way.

Whatever the case, I didn't ask; I just focused on what I needed to do.

From what I saw on television, reporters usually showed up with a pen, paper, and a recording device. Daniel brought a cameraman, an audio assistant, a lighting assistant, and another person whose role was undefined but involved bossing the others around as they tried to stage everything for the interview.

Trinity and I gave them a brief tour of the front rooms, with Jax and Wyatt following closely behind. I wished Theo had stuck around, but he was in damage control mode with the nobles at my own request, so I'd have to catch up with him — on both Charlie and vampire topics — later.

We stuck to the areas that seemed to be the most homey and inviting but saved the library for last, asking if it was the right spot. They agreed enthusiastically, talking about how great the lighting was in all the windows but that they would like to take some b-roll shots around the rest of the property, too.

From across the room, I had to text Trinity to make sure there was a lock on the industrial freezer, and she ran off to confirm. That wasn't necessarily something I was ready for the human population to be privy to quite yet.

"Check, check," one assistant said into the clip-on microphone.

The other nodded and slipped off his headphones to help get Daniel situated with it, running the wire up the back of his shirt before clipping it on his collar. Daniel made himself comfortable on the same leather sofa his son lounged on twelve hours ago.

As they prepped another microphone, I opened the photos app on my phone. There were only a few dozen pictures on the camera roll, but I stared at one of my favorites — the group of humans sitting on the bleachers at Homecoming. Everything seemed so simple back then, even though I was coming to terms with my future and the uncertainty of whether someone was trying to harm me, and I used this picture to help ground me into my humanity.

I didn't expect to be interviewed or broadcasted like this. It wasn't part of the plan, but we needed to do it. The royals, my region, and the rest of the vampires needed me to be more human, and I would do everything I could to make it happen, even if it meant putting myself at the center of it all.

"Mina, we're ready for you," Daniel said, gesturing for me to sit beside him.

How kind of him to invite me to my own furniture. Trinity found the statement humorous, too, judging by the way she unsuccessfully covered her smirk.

The assistant helped me get my microphone set up. He touched my bare skin a few times, which made me uneasy. But I was glad I decided on high-waisted jeans and a button-down instead of a dress.

Once situated, I smoothed my shirt and tried to look natural as I took my seat beside Daniel.

The undefined woman came over and touched up his face with powder, mumbling about how they'd have to fix the shininess in post-production.

I silently asked Trinity if I needed a touch-up as well.

"You're fine, Mina," she reassured me from behind the camera, standing between Jax and Wyatt. "Just try to relax."

"She's right," Daniel said. "This isn't a live broadcast, so I'll ask you questions, and we'll cut the best parts together with the additional footage. I'll probably film the introduction outside your front door, just to give it some additional framing."

"Seems straightforward enough," I agreed.

He grinned while they fiddled with the lighting. It took a few minutes, then they decided they needed an additional light placed behind Daniel before they gave him the thumbs up that they were ready.

Once everyone was in their place with their equipment in hand, it was time to get started.

"Mina, I want to begin this interview by thanking you for having me over to your home," Daniel said. "I can imagine the past twelve hours have been very busy ones for you."

"Thank you for being here, Daniel, and for being so gracious and kind for my first-ever interview. It's a little strange to go from an unknown teenager to all of this overnight."

"You're certainly not some unknown teenager anymore. Last check, you had gained almost two million followers on social media overnight."

"Is it that many? Wow."

Of course, I knew this.

After Isabella outed all of us royals in her interview with CNN, we were getting an overwhelming amount of attention. I immediately stopped bemoaning Jax and Wyatt for their insistence on installing a state-of-the-art security system and beefing up the number of security guards around the property.

But if that wasn't enough, I had Eloise sending me screamy caps text messages every hour with an update on my popularity.

"My son tells me that you're not just a typical vampire," Daniel said.

I hadn't considered what Charlie might have told Daniel about my abilities, being half-human, or being the Queen of Appalachia.

I felt a little guilty at ditching him, once again, last night. The vampire problems triumphed over his human feelings, and he acknowledged it when he texted me early this morning. I struggled to come up with a response, but thankfully, he pivoted the conversation to planning the details of the interview with his father.

I refocused on the words Daniel prompted me with and tried to find a safe response while also showing off my humanity.

"Charlie and I are very good friends," I replied. "We met last fall during our senior year of high school. While I ended up dropping out when my uncle unexpectedly passed away, he and I stayed in touch."

I hoped Charlie didn't mind that I glossed over the truth slightly. He'd forgiven me for a lot, and surely one more thing would slide by him easily enough.

Thankfully, Daniel didn't seem fazed by my response. "Ah, yes, Derrick Byron. I'm so sorry for your loss."

"Thank you." It was my shortest and coldest response yet, and I hoped he would pivot from this topic.

The last thing I wanted to do was reminisce about him with a man who was a thorn in his side.

I wasn't that lucky, though.

"Your uncle was a very important person to our city. His real estate ventures created not only homes but thousands of jobs, and from what I understand, he expanded his business into other industries."

"That's correct. My uncle was a visionary and an

entrepreneur. I learned a great deal from him, and I miss him every single day."

I flicked my gaze over to Trinity, trying to get some confirmation I was doing all right, but she didn't blink. Jax and Wyatt both stayed immovable and imposing beside her while they glared at the humans, as if they were about to torture me.

The interview dragged on for an hour and a half. Daniel asked me probably fifty questions, touching on my background as a half-human, my family, the overnight riots, how vampirism affects humans, how my businesses are helping further vampire-human relations, and several other topics.

I sidestepped questions on my parents, not wanting to explain that I had to banish my own family from my region, and tried to focus on my humanity. It probably would have been too heavy-handed if I ate food on camera.

The assistant suggested we handle the last stages of the interview as we walked through the foyer just to add a little variety. For something that was supposed to be casual, it took even more time to get right than the couch setup.

"So now what?" Daniel asked, his tone as light as I'd ever heard it. "Now that there are vampires roaming freely, what else is going to happen? Are ghosts and goblins going to surface as well?"

I held back a smile. No, just witches and werewolves.

"Ghosts and goblins are the stuff of fairytales, but as you can see, I am a vampire, and I'm walking alongside you."

Daniel laughed and extended his hand. I shook it, and

the assistant made us repeat it a few times so he could get the correct angles.

I followed them around, watching with limited interest as they explored my home further, taking video of my crown, the closet, the kitchen that had been fully stocked with human food before their arrival, the grounds, the cars in the garage, and even the bathrooms.

It felt like a grand intrusion of privacy, but Trinity assured me it helped.

Even though most humans didn't live in a mansion, the everyday items helped show that I was incredibly relatable. I had never been to Isabella's house, but I couldn't imagine it looked anything like mine at this point.

When they finally drove off in the oversized white news van, I breathed a sigh of relief.

Trinity and I both had glasses of blood in celebration, but after the first cheers, I went up to my office, desperately needing some solitude.

"Jax, Wyatt, can you both take a break?" I asked as they followed me in. "I'm sure I'll be fine here for ten minutes alone."

They both nodded and left me to it.

I drained my cup and sat back in my chair, staring at the bright white ceiling.

I'd been going nonstop since Uncle Derrick died, but it hadn't bothered me until the past day. It was easy for me to flitter between meetings, making speeches and decisions, but now that my emotions, my own personal life, were involved...

I felt the pressure of everything on me, as if someone pressed me to the ground and dug their foot in my chest.

I closed my eyes, trying to blacken everything out so I could have a moment of peace to myself, but it failed almost immediately when my phone buzzed with Trinity's name across it.

Your mother has called twice today.

Since following my father into exile, my mother made Trinity the go-between in the few times we spoke.

Is something wrong?

She didn't mention anything. If I had to guess, she wanted to understand how this would impact her and your father.

It shouldn't.

I'll relay that if she reaches out again. Also, you have another video conference shortly with the royals and then a few phone interviews with those publications you earmarked for the rest of daytime.

And then at night I would likely have more meetings with the royals and other vampires, not to mention I needed to address the nobles of the region. It was an endless cycle, and I needed to pull myself together.

I stood up and glanced around at the surroundings, wondering how the hell Uncle Derrick made all of this look so easy.

I moved over toward the chessboard and recalled one of our last conversations over a match where I once again put him in checkmate.

Uncle Derrick picked up the queen, the piece that dealt the final blow. "You know, Mina, in chess, it's the king everyone focuses on, chasing around the board as they inch toward victory, but it's the queen who truly has all the power. Don't forget that."

6

I tried my hardest over the next few days to hold on to those words, and before each meeting and interview to pause, take in fresh oxygen, and try to slow the movement of time.

I can't say it was overly successful, but at least the crisis communication company encouraged us royals that we were making headway, even if it felt like we were answering the same questions over and over. They pulled social listening data and ran polls in partnership with national news sites, showing that more than half of people polled were in favor of us.

"That's better than most presidents," the head of the firm said. "We wanted to let you know that much like we see with alien enthusiasts and UFO chasers, there have been several groups forming around the country in solidarity. In fact, most of them are hoping vampires will show up and turn them."

It didn't entirely make me feel better.

We planned and hoped for a grand unveiling of vampires, with very targeted press announcements and thousands of our kind making themselves known. It was definitely safe to say that things veered off course. There had only been a brave few throughout the country and even fewer around the entire world who had come out.

I supposed part of the hesitation of the others was simply waiting to see the reaction, and so far, it hadn't been exactly promising.

I threw myself entirely to the cause, trying to keep pushing the momentum forward. The more we were talked about — both good and bad — the more "normal" we appeared, which was what we were aiming for at this point. It also helped that Isabella, with her charming personality and beauty, was the face of the movement.

Even though I could relate to humans in my own way, there was something alluring about her, non-threatening, even. Plus, after decades of interactions, the other vampire royals trusted her completely to conduct herself as a queen on camera while pulling in touches of her friendly, more human side — and I guessed I was too much of an unknown to be in that position. Whatever the reason, I was fine with it.

The media training coaches we hired did mention that the rest of the royals needed to work on being more relaxed and less robotic in our responses. The thought of someone like King Isaiah laughing and joking with a reporter made me smile only because I knew hell would have to freeze over before it happened.

Several of my interviews had been published and syndicated, but my piece with the *Gazette* had yet to surface.

As we idled at a red light, I pulled out my phone.

Trinity, can you ask Schenley's people when our interview will publish?

Yes. Will let you know ASAP.

Thank you.

I thought the photos and videos from my home would really help and was eager to see it released, hoping it would resonate with humans.

"We're almost there, your majesty," Jax said, finally turning down a busy street.

It sometimes took him twice as long to arrive at a destination because he took detours and random turns just to make sure we weren't being followed.

I completely pushed the conversation with Theo about Eva's request out of my mind until I saw it on today's schedule. Jax and Wyatt were both uneasy about the situation, but apparently Trinity and Theo had both gone over the logistics with them at length. The twins agreed to wait outside the front doors, staying within earshot if I needed them.

I was grateful all this discussion happened without me, but at the same time, I had a feeling that if Eva didn't want them there, she could have handled it herself with the help of her spellwork. But I didn't think she'd be happy about wasting energy on subduing me *and* two hulking vampires, who insisted on being by my side whenever we left the house.

Plus, the twins tailing me inside would send the wrong message. I needed to build up a rapport with Eva because although she was far from being a threat, I didn't exactly think she was my ally.

We finally pulled up to the apothecary shop, and it was dark enough outside to see the stars overhead. The shop itself was closed for the day, sign facing outward, but Eva instructed me, via Trinity, to let myself in and lock the door behind me.

It was a little eerie in the quiet darkness, but the sweet scent of lavender permeated the air, putting me at ease. I knew it was stupid to feel comforted by the spell that subdues my abilities. But there was something about the buzz that felt familiar and reassuring.

I followed the sound of voices past the stock room and tiny office behind the cash register to the back of the building. And when I stepped into the courtyard, I found myself surrounded by thirteen witches, including Theo and Eva, who all regarded me with various looks of disdain.

Maybe I should have let Jax and Wyatt come with me after all.

"Hello," I said, attempting to greet everyone in the circle at once.

Eva stepped forward, extending a hand that I shook gratefully. "Thank you for coming tonight, Mina."

"Of course." My voice sounded confident, so I added, "I am eager to repay your kindness."

Eva ushered me to a seat and waved at the others to do so before taking her place beside me. The others obliged her request, but they still glanced at me with unease.

"Evaline," one of the older women finally spoke up. Her voice was scratchy in her throat, and her eyes were wide in my direction. "Are you sure this is a good idea?"

Eva didn't hesitate. "Yes," she snapped, glancing at Theo, then me.

I wasn't sure if it was me she wanted to defend or if she needed my help so desperately that she was annoyed someone would object, showing a rift within their community. If they had to turn to vampires, the same species they had to create spellwork to protect themselves from, this couldn't be a simple task.

"Theo mentioned you wanted my help?" I prompted, trying to cut right to the reason she asked me to come by.

"I do, but first, let's have a drink to restore ourselves," Eva said lightly. "And then we'll begin the ceremony."

"The ceremony?" I asked.

My question went unanswered.

We were all given a small silver cup, handed out by the oldest looking witch of the bunch, and I gripped mine warily.

I didn't love being in the dark for what their plans were or what they expected me to drink, but I trusted Theo enough, and Eva slightly, to believe that I wouldn't be harmed.

The witches in the circle chanted — their words were nearly a whisper at first, but by the end of whatever words came out of their mouths, they spoke at full volume.

White smoke rose from the ground, aimlessly moving until each witch flicked a wrist. Just like when Theo controlled the elements in the clearing at my house, somehow they channeled the smoke with their movement, and it dissipated as easily as it came.

They continued, repeating the words I didn't understand, as their fingers delicately traced the rim on their respective cups. Eva moved her thumb along hers and pinky on mine. The movement filled the cups with a dark, thick liquid that came close to overflowing.

The rhythm of the words abruptly stopped, and immediately, the surrounding witches slurped down the liquid. I watched them to see their reaction, making sure it wasn't painful or disgusting to drink.

"It's kind of like tea," Theo mumbled beside me. "We have enhanced it with some elixirs and a few drops of potions, mostly vitamin-based. The others should feel restored by it, but you probably won't be affected by it."

"Oh," I breathed.

"I still recommend you drink it, though, or they'll all take offense."

True to his word, I was being watched by a few around the circle.

I smiled and shot it all back at once, glad I didn't have to hide a grimace. It tasted like honey and mint, with a drop of something else that was extra sweet, a flower, maybe. Following the pattern of those around me, I placed the cup at my feet and turned my attention back to Eva.

"Mina, Queen of Appalachia, we've asked you here today for a purpose," Eva said, and I knew whatever she would say next was as much for me as it was for everyone else. "It starts with a story, one that we're not proud of, but it must be told. Our spellwork demands it, and you need to understand it."

I sat up a fraction straighter, eager to hear what she was going to share.

Even with all of my interactions with Theo, witches were still somewhat of a mystery to me. I hoped that once everything calmed down with the unveiling and human-vampire relations, I could understand more about them, but for now, I'd take in whatever they wanted to share.

"Nearly three hundred years ago, while living in London, one of our ancestors, Mabel, had a run-in with a vampire. Witches were still very much in hiding, protecting themselves in case there were any copycats of the Salem trials in Europe. As we've since learned through her diaries, Mabel took every precaution possible, suppressing her abilities and only using them to create warding spells. As the years dragged on, she grew complacent. She expected to carry out the rest of her life in peace, and she didn't expect to encounter anyone, let alone a vampire, as she tended to her garden on a beautiful summer afternoon."

Eva stopped to pointedly glance around at all the flowers and herbs in the courtyard, as if she could place herself in Mabel's frame of mind.

"The vampire told her he could practically taste her power, but she brushed him off. He didn't like that, of course, after being more than accustomed to getting his way as a vampire. She ran from him as best she could, using every protection spell she had in her repertoire. When she made it to Paris, she tracked down a distant cousin of hers, and together, they crafted a spell that would keep her safe. They were in a rush and unable to discern the complications or anything unexpected that the spell could create. It's no surprise that when he finally tracked Mabel down, the spell didn't perform as planned. She aimed to tie him permanently to the continent while she fled to America. She was successful in doing so, but she also gave him prolonged life."

I gasped. "So the rumor of the three-hundred-year-old vampire in London—"

"Is true," Eva confirmed. "He wasn't able to stalk her across the ocean himself, so over the years, he has sent people to carry out his bidding, and it usually ends with violence. From what research we've been able to do on the spell and our attempts to recreate it from Mabel's diaries, we have all crafted a counterspell that will lift the curse and ultimately kill him, righting the wrong and restoring the imbalance of nature at his existence."

"And what part do I play in this?" I asked. "Protection for when he arrives?"

Theo shifted ever so slightly beside me, and the other witches dropped my gaze.

"We're asking you to find him," Eva said.

My jaw dropped in disbelief. "Excuse me?"

"We would like you to track him down, to subdue him long enough that we can lift the spell, bring him here, and keep him guarded until his life ends."

I nearly sputtered for a response, but remembering what position I was in, and that I was surrounded by a number of powerful witches, I bit my tongue. I rescinded my earlier mental gratefulness toward Eva because this request was legitimately insane.

Uncle Derrick was alive for fifty human years, twenty-two of which he spent as a vampire, and his strength and abilities were impressive, borderline frightening sometimes. I couldn't even imagine what a three-hundred-year-old vampire would be like.

"We will, of course, offer you our own form of protection," Eva assured me coolly. "Which is why we have planned a special ceremony tonight."

I was skeptical of what protection they could offer me from this vampire when they clearly had difficulty protecting themselves from him, or they wouldn't be so determined to end this.

"I haven't agreed to this yet," I said, and part of me knew it was in my best interest to agree to nothing at this point. "This is far beyond a standard ask for protection."

"Your uncle gave his word on our form of payment, no questions asked," Eva reminded me.

Somehow I doubted Uncle Derrick suspected they would put me up to something of this magnitude, especially since we didn't even need her services for the ritual.

"I will need to clear this with the other royals." I told her the only excuse I could come up with at the top of my head. "You may be aware this is somewhat of a busy time for us vampires. Asking me to step away from my duties in the region as well as planning logistics and safety measures for international travel—"

"Of course. I expected nothing less, but we still want to carry on with the ceremony. We want to be prepared for whatever the course of action may be."

Eva said it with such force that I knew I didn't have an option in the matter.

This ceremony, and whatever it entailed, would happen. I would be a part of it. And eventually, I would do whatever else they asked. Deep down, I knew it, but I still tried to at least pretend I had a choice in the matter.

"Let's begin," Eva said, rubbing her hands together in anticipation.

I was the only one who remained seated, and I watched the process of the ceremony with varying degrees of fascination and awe.

They joined hands as they chanted. Once again, their voices started out as a low hum, but as the sound grew, so did their movements. They swayed from side to side as the words turned from speech to a hard, drum-like sound in my ears.

Wind swirled around them, whipping clothes and hair in its wake. They continued on, undisturbed, and I stayed rooted in my chair.

I yelped as the silver cups turned on their sides, clanging against the stones, and rolled into the circle, losing their shape and melting down into liquid at their feet. The smell of burning metal filled my nostrils.

They abruptly dropped hands, tilting their palms to the ground.

In the very slight moments I saw Eva's and Theo's magic, it seemed cloud-like and colorless, but in the night and against the others, I saw the differences. Each person's magic was slightly unique, ranging from deep violet to dark green, and they swirled together, then disappeared into the liquid metal.

The earlier spell had drawn from the elements of earth, but this, whatever they were doing, pulled from the magic inside themselves.

They stopped chanting and held still, watching their magic complete the process. Eva twisted her pointer finger around in circles, shaping the metal to what she desired. Once in a razor-thin circle, like an exposed wire, she leaned forward and blew the air out of her mouth, her mouth a perfect O.

It was as if that motion removed earmuffs from my head because sound returned to normalcy. I picked up on the movement of bugs in the flowers and the panting breaths from the witches.

Eva and Theo usually made spellwork look so effortless, but even with the restorative tea they drank earlier, some of them looked like they were asleep on their feet.

"Mina, step forward, please," Eva said, directing me to the middle of the circle. "Retrieve the talisman."

I did as I was told.

She moved my hands upward, still gripping the metal circle, until she placed it on my head, as if it were my crown and this were some weird witchy coronation. Eva took control, shooing my hands away, and slid the circle down around my skull until the metal touched my neck. She slid my hair out of the way with one hand and traced the metal with the thumb of her other.

Eva muttered a quick incantation, and it shrunk down to act as a choker necklace.

"It's perfect," she said excitedly, admiring the work.

"It is?" I touched it tentatively.

She smiled. "This will protect you and guide you as you fulfill our request."

I appreciated the gesture, but the vagueness of something wrapped tightly around my neck made me feel uneasy.

"How?" I asked while tugging on the metal. It didn't budge.

"We do not know how strong this vampire has become

over time or what abilities he has," Eva explained. "Therefore, we cannot send one of our own kind."

I guessed that was why Theo couldn't carry this out for them. Plus, he was family, and they wouldn't want to put him at any risk.

"Not only does the spellwork carried within it reinforce the shield of your skin, but if you're in peril, we and others of our kind will use it to track you down. Once you find the vampire, we will funnel our spells through this talisman to subdue him, and you will be able to remove it and use it to your advantage, much like the metal chains that are in the basement of your home."

I was completely speechless at the overstepping and, frankly, blind confidence they had in me to carry this out.

"Thank you for considering this, Mina," Eva said, gesturing me forward. "Get in touch with us after you have spoken with the other vampire royals."

"I will," I promised.

I turned back to look at Theo, who refused to meet my gaze as I walked toward the threshold.

In addition to my new piece of jewelry, I walked toward the car with an overwhelming sense of dread.

7

I tried to keep my composure, and hide my neck, on the drive home.

In my attempt to do right by Eva, I made myself stupidly vulnerable, putting blind trust in her and Theo. While their intention might not have been nefarious, I was a little stunned at how casually they put a ring of metal around my neck, one with powers of control I didn't even understand.

My hands shook — from rage or disbelief, I wasn't sure — as I called Trinity.

"How'd it go?" she asked immediately instead of dealing with pleasantries.

"I need you to call an emergency session with the royals."

She paused. "Are you okay?"

Absolutely not.

But I couldn't vocalize that thought or dare fall into my emotions now. I had to be the strong-willed Queen of

Appalachia, defender of vampires and advocate for humanity and not just another teenager who felt overwhelmed and trapped by decisions outside her control.

I forced my gaze out the window, staring at the blurred buildings as we sped toward the mansion.

"I'm messaging with the other secretaries now," Trinity said, accepting my non-response as an answer to her question. "We'll be all set for when you arrive home."

"Thank you," I said, then ended the call.

I could *feel* Jax and Wyatt's concern radiating from them, but I busied myself with trying to collect myself and figure how to explain the grave error I made to the other royals.

I expected they would voice outrage over the entire situation. They were the ones who insisted I needed to be careful and have the near-constant presence of two vampire security guards, but I shunned them and now, essentially, could be controlled by the collar around my neck.

But when I explained to them what happened, what the witches expected, and how it got promised, they seemed pleased, of all things.

"We all are aware of how delicate witch and vampire relations are and have been for the past few hundred years," Mary, the Queen of Plains, said. "Perhaps we could use this as leverage in helping us with our unveiling. Isaiah, didn't you have a witch help you with some conflicts between one of your regional covens in the nineties?"

He nodded. "It was a much faster cleanup than if I had to handle it myself. I am in agreement with Mary. Witches are good to have on our side, Mina. They can help our cause."

It was a good thing I was well-practiced in leaning into my emotionless vampire side because my gut reaction was to yell in frustration. My mental suit of armor was getting too many chinks in it, and soon, I feared I would lose my mind — or at the very least start screaming.

"And you can connect with some European royals while you track the vampire down," Isabella suggested innocently.

I tried to shoot daggers at her through my eyeballs and the screen, but she seemed very smug about the entire thing.

The conversation continued on, with every single royal voicing their support for my helping the witches and connecting with some of our overseas counterparts until I cut them off and agreed to go. I would still need to conduct interviews while there, and the crisis communication firm sent Trinity a lengthy email encouraging me to attend public events and have interactions that would get me photographed.

Jax and Wyatt, of course, would accompany me on the trip, but Trinity would stay behind and take my place in meetings and as the head of the businesses.

The next morning, just as the sun rose, Trinity had me packed, prepared, and ready to go.

I'd never been on a plane before, although Uncle Derrick used helicopters as occasional forms of transportation, but something told me my experience was going to be far from the norm in Isabella's private jet.

I certainly would have never guessed that so soon after

vampires "came out of the coffin," as some headlines said, I'd be setting off to an entirely new country on an errand unrelated to our goal.

The pilot and crew, all humans, were exceptionally nice and welcoming. They'd been working with Isabella for years, apparently, and weren't fazed by the cooler of blood Wyatt carried up the stairs.

In movies and on television, I'd seen plenty of scenes with packed planes and neck pillows, but the small aircraft somehow was spacious and inviting, with its clean white leather upholstery, comfortable couches, and full bathroom at the back of the plane.

Aside from the crew, it was just Jax, Wyatt, and me on the flight, which meant I had their full attention to ask several questions about the aircraft and mechanics of flying before we took off. Eventually, the attendant led us to our seats, instructing us to buckle in and remain seated until we were safely up in the air.

I found the rush of the takeoff and propulsion into the air to be exhilarating, albeit much more comfortable than when Uncle Derrick held me in his arms as he flew upward, but Jax and Wyatt both did not appear to share my sentiment. It was the only time I'd ever seen them break their cool exteriors. Jax gripped the armrest of his chair while Wyatt closed his eyes and mumbled to himself until we reached the cruising altitude.

An attendant came back to our area to ask if we wanted pillows or glasses of blood. I declined both, but I happily followed her instructions to access the internet on my phone.

As I caught up on emails that Trinity triaged for me, my phone buzzed with a text from Eloise.

HELLO, VAMPIRE QUEEN MINA.

This was her new favorite way to address me.

In the days since I told her the truth about me and the news broke to the world, we exchanged a few text messages here and there, which was all I could spare with everything else going on. But now, with five hours of flight time and nothing much else to do, I could catch up.

HELLO, HUMAN ELOISE. How are you?

Charlie and I are about to go to the movies, but you know what I realized?

I frowned. I had yet to actually make it inside a movie theater, get popcorn, and enjoy the experience. It was one of the human activities that stayed at the top of my list to try, and I was a little jealous.

What?

BROOKLYN WAS RIGHT ALL ALONG. HA!

I didn't know if she meant that in a malicious or hilarious way until she followed it up with: *I can only imagine how she is taking this news. I've asked Charlie to call her, but he refuses. Doesn't want to give her the wrong idea, apparently.*

Can't say I blame him.

Anyway, I gotta go. Previews are starting! Sleepover when everything blows over?

Yes, please! I sent, adding a kiss face emoji.

With both Charlie and Eloise out of commission, I had a limited social network of people to chat with. Isabella was swamped with interviews today, but I still took a selfie and sent it to her with a note of gratitude on using the plane. I wish I could have cleared the air with Theo before I jetted off, but if anyone understood where I needed to focus right now, it was him.

Still, I missed how things used to be between us, or at least, what I always imagined they could be. Spending time together, playing chess, talking about the other nobles, exploring more vampire culture…

Before I could think any better of it, I texted him. *Hi.*

The message appeared to deliver, but he didn't respond immediately.

I fished my headphones out of my purse and moved to one of the couches, settling in to watch some YouTube vlogs and tutorials to keep my mind occupied.

The distraction worked. It felt very human and very… me, and I couldn't remember the last time I did this. It felt as if I were stepping backward into a more familiar version of myself. It was like putting on an old comfortable sweater or in my case, my favorite pair of ripped jeans, the ones that Uncle Derrick hated and begged me to burn before I became crowned as the Queen of Appalachia.

Finally, after a few rainbow eyeshadow tutorials, Theo responded. *Hello.*

It was a very formal greeting, and it made me frown.

I didn't just want to pour out everything over text messages. Telling him how much I missed him sounded desperate, and frankly, I still thumbed the choker around my neck uneasily.

I wanted to keep him talking, though.

How are you? I asked.

This time, his response was quick.

Good.

Another one-word answer.

I sighed, and Jax and Wyatt perked up at the sound. "I'm fine," I told them.

Jax went back to reading on his phone, and Wyatt stared out the window, listening to some sports podcast through his headphones that I barely picked up on.

Theo sent another text. *You on the flight?*

Something about him actively engaging in our conversation made me need to sit up and focus on the words. I tried to imagine the deep timbre of his voice instead of the black and gray of the text.

Yes. We took off about an hour ago.

We?

Me, Jax, Wyatt, the crew, the pilots, all the clothes Trinity insisted I needed.

Lol. You still have the talisman?

My hand moved to my neck as I read the words. *I don't think I could take it off if I wanted to.*

True.

That was some spell. Protection AND jewelry all in one.

We kept up the banter for the next hour, talking more about spells, traveling on planes compared to helicopters, Theo's many speeding tickets, what books he had read lately, what Wyatt and Jax were up to at the moment.

My email pinged, a forwarded message linking to the article in the *Gazette* that finally got published. She, kindly, included Theo, the other royal secretaries, and a few other nobles on the chain.

I skimmed through Daniel Schenley's writing. He didn't use the flowery, more magazine-style writing that most articles so far had been using. It read as a pretty straightforward news article, although I perceived a somewhat favorable light on me.

It would probably have been easy for him to create a narrative about me being out of touch with reality, tucked away in my mansion. But he didn't. He spoke with some of my high school teachers who spoke of my work favorably, a member of the city council, and a few employees from the plastic manufacturing company I owned — all who had nothing but positive things to say about me.

The pictures of my home were organized in a slideshow, and I flipped through it twice just to make sure nothing stood out. Trinity must have forwarded him some of my other press photos and a few others from my high school days because they were included in the mix along with some shots from social media.

It was still strange to see myself in the spotlight, and nothing embodied it more than watching myself speak in the ten-minute video. As promised, he picked the best parts of our conversation and spliced clips of my home and us walking over my voice to break up the visuals.

Overall, I was pleased with the piece.

I flipped back to the messaging app, thinking I left Theo hanging mid-conversation, only to see that he was the one who didn't respond to my characterization of Wyatt's very slight but noticeable singalong to whatever musical he asked the attendant to put on for him.

I assumed this meant Theo, too, was reading the article, and I was eager for his reaction to it.

You reading the article? I asked.

Finally, after what felt like an eternity, Theo responded. *Can I ask you something?*

Anything. I meant it.

This entire unveiling and everything. It was for him, wasn't it?

At first I thought he meant Uncle Derrick, but my brain reconciled it with the piece of the article that jumped out. The way I highlighted some parts of my high school experience, my favorite junk food, how I balanced both worlds. Parts of it were very Charlie-centric; although, I tried to use the term "friends" as much as I could.

Not necessarily.

It was an honest response, but I knew I needed to follow it up.

Charlie helped me lean into my humanity, but so did Eloise. And the other humans I interacted with. Uncle Derrick was actually the one who advocated for an unveiling, and at first, I just went along with his wishes. It wasn't until after his death that I realized how necessary it was to ensure the survival of our kind. You are aware of all the benefits for the unveiling, and it was a part of my motivation, but I also believe we should be able to be our truest selves. No hiding anymore.

It was a bit long and preachy, but I hit send on my stream of consciousness.

Okay.

I waited for him to add to it, but he didn't, so I spent the rest of the flight rereading our conversation and fielding texts from Trinity about updates to my schedule for the next few days.

8

Cameras flashed as I walked down the stairs, heading from the plane to the rental car waiting for us on the tarmac reserved for private flights.

Several people screamed questions to me at once, and although my vampire hearing picked up on what they wanted just fine, the human in me did not enjoy being treated like a zoo animal. I kept my mouth shut and head down, letting Jax lead the way.

Once I was in the safety of the tinted windows, the chaos continued. Not just from photographers who followed us and hounded me between meetings, but I barely had time to collect myself and appreciate being in a new country before being whisked away from one place to another.

New scenery, same schedule and problems.

It pleased me to learn that humans in London, and the UK and Europe as a whole, seemed to accept vampires with slight enthusiasm, as opposed to the split reactions in the U.S.

As we drove through the cobblestone streets in the city's heart — on the wrong side of the road by my standards — we passed signs in support and a few rallies welcoming vampires to the mainstream. This was an enormous change from the protests and angry mobs we experienced on July First.

There was something beautifully Victorian and vampire-like about London as a whole, with its rainy weather and architecture. I vowed to come back here on vacation and get lost in as many streets as I could, but it would have to wait until the problems back home, and the issue of the ancient vampire, were dealt with.

That thought to my future self kept me going in the first few days until I met up with Nicholas, Isabella's friend, at her request.

I felt wholly unprepared as I rang the doorbell to his townhouse in a trendy neighborhood of the city called Shoreditch. Isabella didn't fill me in on any of the details of their relationship, and since my last meeting ran over, I hadn't thought to ask Trinity to get it for me until now.

He opened the door and hovered in the frame, eyeing me and my two bodyguards warily.

Most humans and vampires I'd met with politely greeted me with a bow, but Nicholas held himself rigid while his eyes raked over me. I returned the favor, taking in his immaculate black three-piece suit. The shininess of his bald head and the clean, sharp lines of his face only increased the severity of his expression.

"You're it?" Nicholas finally huffed.

I blinked, giving myself a second to confirm I heard that correctly. "Excuse me?"

"The one everyone in the States is going wild over? You're it?"

"You are speaking to the Queen of Appalachia, and you will do so with respect," Jax nearly barked.

He held himself at his full height, as if his stature could intimidate another vampire, but it was only acknowledged with a chuckle from Nicholas, who moved aside and permitted our entry.

"Any other rules I should be aware of?" Nicholas sarcastically asked Jax, who had gone back to his stone-faced self. "Taking orders from Americans in my own home. Hulking ones, at that."

Vampires are severely basic with their possessions, and while Nicholas had sparingly few pieces of furniture, nearly every inch of the house was covered. The walls had framed pictures, prints, drawings, paintings, and newspaper clippings. Books overflowed from the shelf onto the floor, organized into piles by color. Beside them sat about a dozen suitcases, some trinkets and other art pieces, along with stacked boxes.

He produced two chairs out of the disarray, encouraging me to sit. "Blood?" he asked.

It seemed he had manners after all.

"No, thank you," I said with a tight smile.

Even if I needed blood, I didn't necessarily trust the cleanliness of the glass.

He spun his own chair around, like some kind of nineties jock, so he could rest his forearms on the back of the chair while we spoke.

"What is it you need?" Nicholas stared me down.

After days of pleasantries, flattery, and formality, his surliness jarred me. I kind of liked it, though. I wanted answers, not compliments.

"Do you know anything about the rumors of the old vampire around the city?" I asked him.

"You're going to have to be more specific."

"The three-hundred-year-old vampire."

"I do."

I smirked. "Now *you're* going to have to be more specific."

He paused, like he needed to give himself a second to reassess me. "He was always just a rumor until he wasn't. It's a thing in London. Everyone has a story about encountering him, whether they've seen him in passing or watched him tear up a group of vampires—"

"Vampires?" I nearly yelled in disbelief. "He can kill *vampires?*"

I'd never lost myself in a public setting like this before, but I saw the very slight flicker of fear on Jax's and Wyatt's faces.

"He can," Nicholas continued. "He has, and he will probably continue to do so. What else would you do with your time if you were the oldest, most powerful vampire in existence?"

I didn't have an answer for that.

Nicholas's nostrils flared. "We all try to avoid him as best we can, but now that we're all encouraged to come out and just announce ourselves as not humans, what could go wrong?"

"That's why you don't seem to like me very much," I realized aloud.

"Isabella wouldn't shut up about how wonderful you are, about how much good you're doing for our kind." He paused and sniffed the air. "But you're not even truly one of us."

That sneer once would have gutted me, but now, I moved right past it. I had more important things than past insecurities to focus on.

"Where can I find him?"

Nicholas's gaze shifted to utter disbelief.

"The vampire," I pressed. "Do you know where he lives?"

"You're going after him?"

I didn't bother justifying his question with an answer. He had made his opinion of me clear, and he didn't deserve an explanation. "Do you have any information about his whereabouts?"

"You can't just waltz up to him and ask him if he wants a glass of blood," Nicholas said. "What do you plan on doing when you find him? Asking him nicely to stop killing vampires?"

"That is of my concern, not yours."

Nicholas stood up, moving to stare out the window while he spoke. "Take the train to Brighton. Leave the station and walk in the direction of the pier. You'll no doubt pick up on the scent of vampires, eventually."

"He'll be there?" I clarified.

Nicholas shrugged. "Doubtful, but if anyone can help you, it's the coven there."

I pulled out my phone to text Trinity with the update in

our plans. "Thank you," I said to him kindly, even though he didn't deserve it.

As we left, Jax slammed the door so hard that the windows on the front of the house completely shattered.

Although the train would have taken us on a faster, more direct route down to the coast of England, Jax and Wyatt argued for the safety and flexibility of driving, and I didn't put up a fight.

Instead, I sank back in the seat and fired off a text to Isabella. *Just met Nicholas.*

Her response was immediate. *And???*

I rolled my eyes even though she couldn't see the motion. *You could have warned me about him.*

And spare myself of whatever you're going to tell me about your visit? Not a chance.

He's an arrogant prick.

I'm familiar.

How did you say you knew him again?

She sent several laughing face emojis. *From my human days. We had a loooot of wild nights together in college.*

"Gross," I said aloud with a disgusted tone and added, "I'm fine," before either Jax or Wyatt could ask from the front.

I'm going to forget you said that.

HA! I'll be sure to send you all the details later.

Please, please, please, do not.

As we drove, I kept my gaze fixed outward, mesmerized by small things like the differences in road signs and how the air changed as we moved closer to the water.

Uncle Derrick traveled sporadically, mostly for working on overseas business deals but occasionally to meet with human politicians and other vampire royals. He always made it a point to bring something back for me, usually of the chocolate variety. I wished I had time to explore some places he'd visited, but I needed to maintain my focus on the task at hand.

A very large part of me expected that Nicholas set us up for failure, but as his instructions indicated, we found the group of vampires easily enough.

It definitely helped that instead of being cooped up in some luxurious building, they were all congregated on the rocky beach.

If I didn't know — or couldn't smell — better, I would have assumed it was a gaggle of humans, relaxing and enjoying a vacation complete with beach chairs and multiple umbrellas. They sat casually, wearing sunglasses and hats, as if their bodies were impacted at all by the currently overcast sky.

We approached downwind, giving me the chance to eavesdrop before they picked up on my scent.

"I heard that soon, they're going to sell blood bags in Sainsbury's."

"Imagine that, having to decide between blood types while humans just mill about buying produce and such."

"Well, I for one am enjoying the circus around it."

"Say, do you smell that, it's like—" She abruptly stopped, then turned to face me directly.

I held my hands up defensively, assuring her we weren't here to cause any problems. Jax and Wyatt stood so close that they almost touched me as we stopped our approach.

"Hello," I said confidently.

Her eyes raked over my appearance and the twins beside me. "You're Mina, aren't you? Queen Mina of…"

"Appalachia," I finished for her.

"Right then."

The entire group stood, bowed, and resumed their casual positions in their beach chairs before I could assure them it was unnecessary. But like the many differences between here and home, they actually still respected monarchy and traditionalism.

"You're quite a long way from home, your majesty," she said. "What can we do for you?"

"I was told you could help me get in touch with the three-hundred-year-old vampire."

At this, they all went silent, exchanging quick glances among one another.

Another vampire finally spoke up. "We have nothing to do with him, your majesty."

I folded my arms across my chest, a show of me definitely not believing his insistence. It was a very human thing to do, and they all noticed.

"I am asking for your help," I said to the group, ignoring his remark. "I am here, with limited time, on a very specific errand. A vampire, trusted by the American royals, told me you could provide me some guidance in tracking down the oldest known vampire."

No one moved or spoke up, which chipped away at my patience level.

Realistically, even though they were light and accepting of the unveiling here in England, they were likely reluctant to stick their necks out — for anyone, let alone some foreign royal.

"I'll use discretion when I finally track him down. No one from your regional royalty knows I'm here with you now. The sooner I'm provided with answers, the sooner I'll be gone." I offered a sideways glance at Jax and Wyatt, trying to channel some of their intimidation skills. "Or I'll stay, but I don't think you'll want that."

It was clear that was absolutely what they did not want, but I wasn't sure if it was because I would attract attention to them or that they didn't want to deal with the pomp and circumstance of bowing and politeness.

Several voices spoke at once.

"We haven't seen him in about three months."

"Sometimes he stays for a year, other times he is gone in a few days."

"He's so shifty."

"He's quite old looking, but don't let his exterior fool you."

"His power is like nothing I've ever seen before."

"And he has his own set of rules and morals dictating how he uses it."

I held up my hands as a signal for them all to stop talking, and they obliged me.

"Can anyone tell me his name?" I asked.

They gave me no response.

"You've interacted with him a number of times and have no idea what he calls himself?"

"It isn't so much interacting as we just try to help him with whatever he needs in hopes that he'll leave again soon."

"And you have no way to contact him?"

The first female vampire who addressed me spoke up

again. "No, your majesty, but I have heard he frequents the cities around Paris, and he also spends quite a bit of time in southern Spain."

"Okay then," I said. "I appreciate all of your time and information. If you think of anything else, please reach out to me through the proper channels."

I didn't wait for them to bow to me once more; I sped off as fast as I could to debrief with Trinity and change our travel plans.

9

Every flight is grounded out of Heathrow at the moment because of a patch of summer storms just west of London.

I groaned at Trinity's text message.

Might as well stay at the hotel for now. Even if the storm clears, they're prioritizing cargo and large passenger jets.

I looked out the window to see light traffic navigating just fine through the sprinkle of rain. From my vantage point, I saw people milling about, some not even using umbrellas as they laughed and walked.

Most men wore too-tight blue suits with crisp white shirts unbuttoned at the top, the apparent uniform for eligible bachelors in London. The differences in fashion were slight in comparison to their personalities, the volume at which they speak, and the little intricacies while doing so compared to humans back home. It was fascinating to me to hear all the different accents, even within one city.

My region touched seven states in the U.S., and while

there were little things that differed in the way some words were spoken and vowels enunciated, the people in this city seemed to be speaking other forms of English entirely. Maybe if I understood more about these humans, I'd have a better understanding of why they were so much more accepting of vampires than those in the United States.

I wanted to walk among these humans, listen in on their conversations, and maybe even interact with them. But I wasn't here on vacation or my own personal errand; I was a vampire queen, locked up on the third floor of a gaudy hotel, waiting for the weather to clear out so we could chase an ancient vampire around Europe.

Of course, Jax and Wyatt would oblige me if I wanted to go for a walk outside. They wouldn't like it — there were too many people out at the moment — and the thought of them trailing behind me, intimidating and capturing the attention of the humans ruined the allure for me.

It was absurdly selfish and definitely not fitting of the persona I'd built for what I thought the Queen of Appalachia should be.

But for even ten minutes, I wanted to be a completely anonymous, boring teenager walking through a new city on her own. That thought flooded my mind with feelings of lightness and excitement, and it terrified me that I couldn't recall the last time I allowed myself to experience those emotions.

I had to go for it and escape from this stifling existence momentarily to regain my independence and a shred of sanity.

Through the crack of the bedroom door, I watched Jax and Wyatt sitting together on the couch, both concentrating on their phones. I crossed the room, slowly and naturally, toward the bathroom. When we first checked in, I thought it was ridiculously extravagant given that we'd spend most of our time outside the hotel, but now, I felt grateful to have another door and a television mounted on the wall to help muffle the sound.

I closed the bathroom door and locked it behind me, knowing that even though Jax and Wyatt could break through it easily enough if needed, they would assume I needed a little privacy.

To muffle the sound of my escape, I ran the faucet on the tub, then flipped the latch on the window. I don't know what human would want to sit naked in front of a giant window with sheer blinds, but it worked out for me now.

As quietly as I could, I slipped out onto the window ledge and shimmied myself down.

When my feet hit the cobblestone courtyard, I felt an overwhelming sense of accomplishment. It was pathetic, really, considering I used to climb much greater heights out of sheer boredom during the late nights when I lived with my parents. Back then, I didn't have a crown, two vampires attuned to my every move, and a desperate need for solitude.

I realized too late that in my haste to leave, I didn't bring my phone or my purse, meaning I had no way to pay for tea I wanted to try or souvenirs I wanted to bring back. I frowned at that momentary lapse of judgment, as if this entire endeavor wasn't one, shook off the thought, and started walking.

I found London to be a little overwhelming, but in the best way possible. Walking through the streets was like being in a dream at the intersection of history and modernism. Humans tuned out the world around them with their headphones while breezing past a pub that looked like it was straight from the early twentieth century. Double-decker buses whizzed by, making somewhat abrupt and terrifying turns in too-small roadways, while my mind worked on overload trying to process everything.

In short, I loved it.

I wouldn't have even noticed that the rain picked up around me had it not been for the increase in panicking humans around me. I laughed at how some of them scrambled to cover their hair with their purses or newspapers if they didn't have an umbrella.

I just soaked it in, leaning back against an exposed exterior stone beam of a coffee shop as a crack of lightning hit far above the city.

I counted in my head until the thunder sounded and thought of Theo, just like I did every time it stormed, remembering the way the sweet smell of the fresh, wet air swirled around us in my car.

A streak of lightning lit up the sky, distracting me as I drove. Theo counted under his breath until a jolt of thunder sounded.

"Eleven," he whispered.

I turned off the music. "Eleven?"

"When I was a child, my mom said if you count between the lightning and the thunder and divide by five, that's how many miles away the lightning struck."

"Why would you need to know that?"

"I don't know. I don't even know if it's accurate, but it's just something I've always done."

Since then, it became something I always did, too.

The little moments in life were the ones that stuck out to me most — small smiles, brief conversations, gestures of kindness, and ones that made me feel so close to humanity. That moment was the first time a vampire had ever really spoken fondly of their humanity, and it was such an innocent declaration on Theo's part, one of the last, normal conversations we had before everything changed.

After that car ride, and that kiss in the rain, I wanted to go tell Charlie everything, but fate, or something like it, intervened. Instead, I chased Daniel Schenley to a crime scene, and everything snowballed after that into my father's truth, Uncle Derrick's death, and my coronation.

That one jolt of electric blue lightning and everything changed.

Crack.

The sound of lightning snapped in my ears. I wiped the warm drops from my face and blinked, causing the blurry faces around me to come into focus.

These people, surprisingly, weren't rushing toward their destination and avoiding the rain. At first, I didn't see the coordination in their movements because they were spread out on the block, but now that I focused on it, I saw the same look of determination across their faces.

The rain had masked the scent and haze of magic that blanketed each individual witch with protection.

A tall woman with a remarkable resemblance to Evaline stepped forward. "Inside, please," she said politely, gesturing to the doors to my left.

I unleashed a string of curse words in my mind.

The rational part of me should have been afraid, but when I stepped inside and was met with the familiar lavender scent and thickness of the air, I relaxed a fraction, confirming my suspicion that I was probably the only vampire in existence who was encouraged and comforted by magic that attempted to subdue them.

Still, I was surprised when the woman gestured for me to sit beside her on a comfortable-looking sofa, as if we were old friends. It wasn't exactly that she abducted me, but given that I had the talisman around my neck, and was in the presence of multiple witches, I didn't think I had much free will at this point.

"I'm Maggie," the woman said.

"Mina," I offered out of politeness and possibly insanity.

She laughed. "Of course, I know who you are."

That was obvious, unless they made a habit of cornering vampire royalty on the streets.

"Evaline is my cousin," she said. "Well, maybe my second cousin? Once removed?" She waved off the calculation in her mind. "Doesn't matter."

The others joined us, setting a pot and a tray of pastries on the table in front of us. I inhaled, appreciating the slight hint of citrus in the tea and the sugary, buttery scent from the scones.

Maggie and the others jumped in, pouring the hot liquid into their teacups and trying to decide which baked goods they wanted to eat. And I couldn't resist doing so, too. They hadn't exactly offered, but this was my chance to experience the taste of London, and I would not miss it.

I sniffed the tart discreetly before I nibbled on the edge. It was some sort of lemon custard topped with a fruit jam — fig, maybe — and it was pretty pleasant along with the flaky sweetness of the crust.

I swallowed it, glancing up at the others in time to realize that they hadn't actually expected me to partake in their afternoon tea.

"Oh, sorry," I said, setting the tart down on one of the napkins, as if someone would want to eat a tart with a few vampire teeth marks in it.

"How… you can eat?" Maggie asked.

I nodded. "I'm half-human, half-vampire," I explained, flicking the crumbs from my fingers onto the napkin with precision. "Did Eva not mention it to you?"

"'Eva,' is it?" Her laughter echoed through the silence.

She was surprised by the familiarity of her cousin and me, which made me believe I made a grave mistake in not using my vampire strength and speed to get away from the witches as quickly as I could. Now, of course, that wasn't an option. I couldn't even release my fangs from my gums if I wanted to.

"I assumed she told you I would be here?"

Maggie took a sip of her tea, holding the saucer in her hand while she did so, making me realize that my favorite oversized mug at home would look tacky as hell in this setting.

"We haven't spoken in quite a while," Maggie explained. "I didn't intend to mislead you when I said I recognized you. Surely you know that you've crossed over into our tabloids as well?"

At the suggestion of the crisis communication company, the secretaries of the royals made it a point to keep a running list of every press mention featuring one of us. After the first thousand links, it became too much for me to keep track of, so I asked Trinity to send me a daily round-up of the ones that stuck out to her.

I couldn't recall anything specific from overseas publications. "I've seen a few mentions here and there."

"It's like we've gotten a second wave of royalty to pay attention to and scandalize. Who knows what would happen if us witches revealed ourselves as well?" She smiled wryly at the thought. "But I digress. I brought you here for a very specific reason."

"And what was that?"

"To find out what you're doing here."

I laughed. It was somewhat involuntary, but once again in London, I found myself completely surprised.

At least in the region, I had Uncle Derrick's advice or Trinity's experience and knowledge to go off, but here, it was like sidestepping landmines. First with Nicholas's personality, then the vampires of Brighton, and now, these witches. Honesty had done well so far, so I kept it up.

"I'm here to find the three-hundred-year-old vampire," I said.

To drive the point home, I tapped on the talisman on my neck, hoping she would sense the magic and meaning behind it.

Their surprise was more palpable than it was when I bit into the tart.

Every single witch in the room shifted closer to me, trying to get a better look at the metal on my neck. Maggie, who was sitting a comfortable distance away at the start of our conversation, practically dove on my lap to get closer to it.

"Well, that's something, isn't it?" Her eyes didn't leave

my neck as she scooted backward, giving me some of my personal space back.

"It is, I suppose."

"Tell me, Mina, what exactly did Evaline tell you about this vampire?" Before I could answer, she waved her hand in my direction. "Don't answer that because I know she told you a version of the truth. Or at least, enough to get you over here." She paused and took another long sip of tea. "So let me tell you the actual truth, and we'll compare notes."

"Fair enough," I agreed.

"Mabel was Evaline's great-great-grandmother, and the witch in Paris, the one who helped her create the protection spell, was mine. I'm sure she told you about the complications of the spell, how it accidentally prolonged the vampire's life. The thing is, he wasn't supposed to stay trapped here... that was an addition Mabel put in, knowing that it would keep him here and endangering anyone who stayed behind."

"And I'm assuming Mabel already had plans to leave?"

"Got on a ship and left a note behind," she said in a clipped tone. "We've been living in fear ever since."

"You don't want to just leave?" I asked, genuinely curious.

Maggie frowned at this suggestion. "Our protection spells, as weak as they are at the moment, are working to keep the entire witch community safe," she explained. "What would happen if I just got up and left my home? Aside from that, why should I be the one to leave? And pay the price for someone else's mistakes?"

I tried to imagine what it would be like if, say, Trinity

jeopardized my safety like that. If she deceived me so completely and then fled, only leaving a note behind, would I want to leave with her? Probably not — especially if it meant giving up my home, the same one Uncle Derrick shared, and leaving it to fall apart.

"The only satisfaction I get out of all of this is that the vampire still terrorizes Mabel's direct bloodline from afar," Maggie added.

Her callousness contrasted the proper persona I built for her in my mind, but at least she was being direct with me.

"How so?" I asked.

"You've heard about his unnatural strength?"

"That he can kill vampires?" How could I forget?

"I've also heard he has powers of influencing people around him," Maggie said. "Getting people to do what he wants them to do. I don't know if that's accurate, but over the years, there have been a few known attacks on the witches of that bloodline."

I blinked. "I haven't heard of that."

"Because why would witches want you vampire royals to know that they're vulnerable? One happened recently, actually, Evaline's nephew, I think. Although, for whatever reason, the vampire turned him instead of killing him."

"Theo?" I nearly screamed.

Maggie's eyebrow raised. "You're familiar then?"

The oldest known vampire *hunted* Theo down.

I was so furious I was speechless, and because of their magic, my body couldn't physically react. My fangs stayed put in my gums, and the anger simmered beneath my skin, causing me to twitch. I had to sit on my hands to stop from freaking out.

To her credit, Maggie gave me a minute to compose myself before she delivered the worst blow yet.

"So that's why she sent you to do it," she said, piecing together everything aloud. "The moment her bloodline crosses the Atlantic, the protection is broken. And now that vampires are 'out' in the world, there's nothing to stop him or anyone else from traveling anywhere."

She gave me a once-over.

"Especially with the endless resources and opportunities when befriending a queen."

So they used me.

I knew that, somewhat, going into this entire ordeal, but it made complete sense to me now. They wanted to protect their own, even if it meant endangering me.

With all this new information, I was a little ashamed of the most pressing question in my mind: Did Theo know all of this?

Because, essentially, with the strength and power of this vampire, I had the slimmest of chances in being able to pull out my phone, get in touch with the witches, and have them activate the subduing magic in my talisman. I was willing to risk it in honor of the favor we owed Eva, but now, with this additional insight from Maggie and what I'd learned since arriving… I wasn't so sure.

Maggie took another sip of her tea. "The most unfair of it all is that if she had enough power to confine him to a location, she should have taken the time to, I don't know, trap him in a cellar or something."

"Do you know where he is?" I asked. "Vampires in

Brighton told me he was likely somewhere in France at the moment."

"Every full moon we're able to do a location spell, and last we checked, he was in southern Spain."

I stood, hoping that she and the others would give me permission to leave. "Thank you for your help and the information, Maggie."

She stood up, not to stop me but in curiosity and possibly slight panic. "You're not still going after him, are you?"

"I'm not sure yet," I admitted. "Is this your establishment?"

"Been in the family for over fifty years," she said, walking me over to the door like we'd just had a light conversation about the weather.

"I'll reach out with what my plans are soon, once I reconcile all of this additional information and talk to the other royals." I addressed everyone in the room, who all offered me looks of awe and shock, before I stepped outside. "Take care, and thank you for your hospitality."

I sprinted, not bothering to slow myself down to normal human speed, back to the hotel.

I nearly cried with the release of my fangs and how good it felt to no longer defy my nature as I scurried back up the wall and into the bathroom. The tub was drained, and the door was open enough for me to hear Jax and Trinity on the phone.

"She's back," he said, making his way over to me.

I saw the pure rage in his expression, and I was a little curious if he was going to scold me, which was well deserved but hardly appropriate. But I didn't give him the chance to. Instead, I tore the phone out of his hand.

"Trinity, change of plans," I told her.

"What happened, Mina? Where have you been?"

I ignored her questions and the two vampires in front of me who were furious at my disappearance. "We're going to the airport now. It doesn't matter if we need to hide in cargo crates or whatever, we need to get back home as soon as possible."

10

When we finally arrived back home to the mansion, it felt like it had been a month since I left.

Departure delays and rude people will do that to a person, I guess, but eventually, we wrangled the airport staff and were able to jet off rather quickly once the storms passed.

The time and distance combined with restlessness made me fidget the entire flight back. My movements were, apparently, annoying enough that Jax and Wyatt moved to the back part of the plane, something they probably would have endured under normal circumstances, but I could tell I still wasn't totally off the hook for sneaking out.

It was worse when I filled them and Trinity in on the details.

Repeating what I learned to them didn't help quell my rage, and the more I thought about it in the air, my emotions morphed into something between fury and resentment — the lines were definitely blurred between the two.

As we pulled up the long driveway, I was pleased to see Theo's outrageous yellow sports car parked in the front. I asked Trinity to ensure Theo and Eva were both at the house when I arrived, but I wasn't sure if she'd be able to convince them.

In fact, in my mind, it was somewhat of a test.

If they insisted I come to the apothecary shop, where the magic subdued me, they knew what I discovered and were prepared to answer for it. This, however, told me they had no idea because, obviously, Trinity wouldn't give them any details before I arrived.

"Welcome home," Trinity said as she opened the front door for us.

I was genuinely happy to see her again, but I needed to take care of this before I could focus on greeting her properly.

"I set out some blood for you," she called as I sprinted up the stairs.

"Thank you!" I yelled over my shoulder.

I threw open the double doors, causing Eva to jump — she didn't have the superpowered vampire hearing Theo and I had; although, his was far better than mine.

In this situation, Uncle Derrick would have been calm and calculated. I imagined his cool demeanor, so nonchalant and unrevealing, so vampiric. I wasn't sure if it was because I was half-human or if I was just *that* angry, but when I stormed in, I didn't accept their greetings; I bolted right to the bar setup in the corner where Trinity left two bags of blood and my mug out for me.

Turning toward Eva, making sure she could see the spikes of my fangs, I dug them into the plastic, sucking down the blood easily from the first bag and repeating the motion on the next. I kept my eyes on her as I did it, purposely trying to make her uncomfortable, and when she averted her gaze, I knew I was successful.

"You didn't find him, I take it," Theo finally spoke up.

I tossed the bags down, wiped a few droplets of blood off my chin with the back of my hand, and took a step toward them, keeping my focus on Eva.

She braced herself for my next words by wrapping her arms around herself, shifting from the powerful and fierce witch to a small and fragile woman. It was a simple movement in her body language to call to my instincts to back off, and I stared at her, mouth open, wondering how many other little ways she'd manipulated me.

Her lips moved slightly, chanting words to bubble up protection around her and Theo, while she waited to see what I would do next.

I had blind faith in her, wanting to help someone who seemed so frightened — or maybe it was because of Theo — and I regretted it.

My display of blood already had her a little pale and off-kilter. Coming at her with the full force of my anger wouldn't do any of us any good, even though the temptation was there. Outright attacking her would be a horrible mistake. After all, she had the upper hand in the form of the talisman around my neck.

I moved over toward the window, looking out into the trees to help ground me, just like Uncle Derrick used to do.

"You lied to me," I said, trying to swallow the anger as best I could.

"What did you say?" Theo had the gall to ask.

I turned back, meeting his eyes. "You. Lied. To. Me."

"When?" Theo asked, brows furrowed. "For what?"

About thirty different things, but I went with one of the simplest ones. "You told me Philip turned you."

Theo relaxed his posture, assuming I was having some grand overreaction to something so arbitrary. "No, you assumed it, and I didn't correct you. He *found* me afterward, but he didn't turn me."

"You're really going to argue semantics with me right now?" I balked. "Keeping me in the dark on all of this, Theo, it's unacceptable. The danger you knowingly put me in..."

He seemed genuinely confused. "What are you talking about?"

Theo, exasperated, turned to Eva for confirmation that I was speaking out of turn, but as his gaze dropped to her shaking hands, he seemed taken aback. This, thankfully, confirmed that he had absolutely nothing to do with the real reason why she sent me over.

That revelation made me a little relieved — but no less angry at her.

"He doesn't know," I snapped, directing my tone at Eva. "You haven't told him any of it?"

She chewed on her bottom lip, trying to find the right words. "Theo wanted to take you on a surprise trip to Paris after your coronation."

Maggie's explanation came to the forefront of my mind.

The moment her bloodline crosses the Atlantic, the protection is broken.

"Apparently, you mentioned a chocolate shop once, and he thought it would be some grand gesture," she said, nostrils flaring in annoyance.

Her tone and demeanor were the exact opposite of the gesture's sweet intention, and Theo looked embarrassed by her admission, not wanting something so thoughtful and personal broadcasted — especially since he didn't go through with it.

"Obviously, I talked him out of it," she admitted with a shrug. "You have been too busy to celebrate anyway, but I had to take precautions in case he had ideas in the future."

My mind reeled, but I pressed on. "So you lied to us both, potentially sending me out to slaughter and keeping him in the dark. Seems like a foolproof plan, Eva."

"What the hell is going on?" Theo demanded, his magic crackling at his fingertips in anger.

"Do you want to tell him, or should I?" I asked Eva, who gave me no response. "I met Maggie, one of your relatives in London, and a few other witches. They told me the *truth* about this errand and ancient vampire."

Theo crossed his arms on his chest, a very human move that endeared me to him even as he snapped at me. "Which is?"

"That your distant relative Mabel is responsible for everything that went wrong with the spell. She fled to the U.S. and left her entire family in danger to deal with the fallout. If anyone in Mabel's bloodline crosses the Atlantic, the spell is broken, meaning he can hunt you down. But, don't worry, that doesn't matter necessarily because this vampire apparently can *kill* and *influence* other vampires, sending his minions over here to do the work for him."

I paused, ensuring Theo's attention stayed on my every word.

"And that is why you were turned. Revenge."

Theo blinked, taking in my words, then in a flash, he stood menacingly over his beloved aunt. "Is it true?" Theo demanded.

"Yes," she said simply. "But there's more."

"Of course there is," I sighed, rolling my eyes.

She glared at me. "You're connected to this, too."

"Other than you sending me across the ocean with half-truths?"

She ignored the jab and reached into her purse. "There's this," she said, holding up a small glass bottle.

I snatched it out of her hand and traced the jagged lines on the olive green glass.

The first and last time I held this bottle, Uncle Derrick and I sat in the backseat of the car. He told me I was going to have to drink the blood inside it as part of the vampire ritual, and I was not looking forward to it.

Although we did change our plans, I never thought to ask Trinity where the bottle went. "Why do you have that?" I asked her.

"This," she turned to Theo, "is the blood of Jonathan, the first King of Appalachia. For all intents and purposes, he was Mina's great-great-grandfather. Had we gone forward with the sacred ritual last fall, Mina would have drank this blood, which was believed to offer protection."

"Uncle Derrick told me that," I admitted.

"But what he didn't tell you, likely because he didn't

know, is the reason the witch agreed to spell the blood and keep it alive was because Jonathan and Eliza were the ones who helped Mabel escape and start a new life in America."

"But I thought they weren't turned until they arrived?"

"Correct, and they were hunted down by one of the ancient vampire's proteges, who fell for Eliza immediately and turned her, hoping to change her affection. Obviously, it didn't work, but before Eliza turned Jonathan, the witch agreed, in exchange for their help, to create a spell for all Eliza's descendants."

"But you knew I didn't take it, and you still let me go."

She shrugged. "You and King Derrick were adamant about not moving ahead with the ritual, so I improvised," she said, gesturing to the metal choker on my neck.

"Then why do you have it now? Why the blood?"

"This blood has Mabel's magic in it. I planned to use it to help get rid of the vampire once and for all. I'm not nearly as powerful as the witches before me, like we have discussed before with the metal chains in your home. We'll need something stronger to kill this vampire."

"Then do it," I told her. "Create the weapon, and I will bring it with me."

She shook her head. "You will need a witch to wield it."

"I'll go," Theo cut in.

I'd been so enthralled with the story and the back and forth with Eva that I was momentarily spared from how Theo was reacting to this. His fangs were still tucked away, but his body shook with anger.

Eva shook her head. "You can't, Theo. It will break the—"

"I said I'll go." The finality in his tone was clear.

Eva held the glass to her chest. "I can't let you do that, Theo. You're my family, and I need to keep you safe—"

"By lying to me about it?" Theo seethed. "By letting me believe some random vampire turned me and that I was needed here to help you when you sent Mina off on her own, relatively clueless? I can barely look at you right now, Eva. I don't even have the words right now to explain how betrayed I feel."

Eva reached out for him, but he turned away.

She swallowed, giving herself a moment to blink away the tears pooling in her eyes. "Theo, I was devastated enough when you turned," she drawled, voice thick with emotion. "Imagine what will happen when vampires learn that witches still keep their power when they become vampires. Who knows what he'll do to you if you fail!"

The line of his jaw hardened. "Well, then I guess we'll find out."

Eva's eyes went wide. "I-I need time to get the spell ready."

"Mina, is twelve hours enough time to update the royals and make arrangements for travel plans?" Theo said, unable to look at me as he spoke.

"Yes," I said, already rapidly firing off texts to Trinity.

"I'll inform the nobles and return here by sunrise," Theo said, leaving Eva and me in an angry standoff until she stomped off behind him.

11

Jax and Wyatt eyed Theo warily.

Perhaps they sensed the awkwardness between us and wanted to show their support for what I'd gone through or — in all likelihood — they didn't entirely trust him because of Eva's deception.

It was unfair of them to lump Theo in the same category, making broad generalizations against him because of his family. It would be the same unkindness if people likened me to my father's mistakes or even held me up to Uncle Derrick's high standards and business savvy. I was my own person, and although they both influenced me growing up, my decisions now stood on their own.

Just like how Theo, agreeing to come and help despite the tremendous risk, was equal parts brave and reckless — but it was his choice.

To Eva's credit, now that everything was seemingly cleared up with the complicated history of humans, vampires, and witches in this instance, she complied with Theo's order and hand delivered the weapon to me herself.

Her spell transformed the bottle into a small glass dagger with the blood swirling around on the inside. She assured me it was unbreakable in its current state and that the spell, wielded by Theo and assisted by the talisman around my neck, would kill the vampire.

I wasn't exactly keen to believe her wholeheartedly again, but just like the metal around my neck was her insurance policy, having Theo with me, unfortunately, was kind of my own. I couldn't trust her to value my life, but I figured she wouldn't want any harm to come to him.

In short, direct messages back and forth, Theo and I agreed we would start our vampire hunting in Madrid, then work our way to the southern coast of Spain. Part of me wanted to stop in London so he could meet Maggie and the others in person, but it was best to just follow their advice. Along the way, we wanted to try to connect with as many vampires and witches as we could find until we hopefully tracked down the vampire.

We were all set to go — until the royals changed our course of action.

While they still believed it was in the best interest of vampires to have the witches on our side, they asked me to make a quick pit stop.

Most protests had died out around the country, but there was an emergency assembly at the United Nations building in New York that they wanted Isabella and me to be present for. And since I would be in the media center of the world, they lined up a bunch of interviews as well to maximize my time before I set off across the ocean once again.

Given how much I loved London, I couldn't say I was too terribly disappointed about having time in another gigantic city — even if it just gave me more time to get nervous over finding the ancient vampire.

I assumed Theo would wait to join until we were ready to depart for Europe, but he was already on Isabella's plane when Jax, Wyatt, and I boarded for our flight to LaGuardia. Trinity must have given him the information, and as I was texting her to ask about it, she messaged me first.

Eloise just stopped by the house.

I sighed, wishing I had more time with her before she went off to college in the fall. I didn't have time to update her on everything that was happening, but I texted her when I was on the way back from London, and we had a quick back and forth.

I'll call her.

She's moving into her dorms in less than a month. I put it on the calendar for you.

Thank you, Trinity.

Once we reached cruising altitude, I stepped into the bathroom and dialed Eloise. I think it was frowned upon by the human pilots, and the vampires on the plane would pick up on the conversation, due to their hearing and the confined space, but I was happy to have the illusion of privacy and went ahead with it, anyway.

"Where have you been?" Eloise asked, not bothering with the typical pleasantries of a phone call. "And where are you right now?"

"I think I'm a few thousand feet over Clarion," I told her.

"You're calling me from the airplane?"

"More specifically, the airplane bathroom."

She laughed. "I didn't realize life as a vampire queen was so glamorous."

"What are you up to?" I asked.

"Watching garbage television, of course. But in fifteen minutes, the first *Legally Blonde* movie starts."

Her response was so normal, and I missed being normal — or at least, I missed the days where conversations didn't revolve around scheduling, blood, killing vampires, and my region.

Once this was all over, I wanted to spend an entire week doing the most boring human things possible. I just hoped it would happen sooner rather than later, as I didn't know how busy Eloise would be with college in the fall.

I frowned at the thought.

I was ecstatic when she told me she earned a decent scholarship to Carnegie Mellon. She planned to double major in finance and business to be a "badass rich boss," as she put it.

She would only be a car ride away, but things would change. She'd get swept up in classes, homework, and new friends, and I'd be dragged more and more into the vampire world.

I was being selfish, but I wanted to monopolize her time while I could.

"Well, instead of that, how about you pack a bag and join me in New York City?" I asked her.

"What?" she exclaimed.

It sounded like she upturned her bowl of snacks onto the floor.

I laughed. "I never got you a graduation gift, so how about I get you a plane ticket and you can come here for a few days? I can't promise it will be much fun, but you can go off on your own and explore if you want while I'm in interviews and meetings."

"Why are you acting like you have to convince me of anything?" Eloise snapped. "New York City with my best friend? How soon can I get there?"

"I'll have Trinity set you up with everything once we get off the call."

She squealed in the background, and although I didn't make a sound, I shared that sentiment. Not only was I genuinely excited to spend time with her but the idea of making her feel this way made me happy, a rare emotion these days.

"Okay, okay, I'll start packing now! Oh my gosh, what the hell am I going to wear? Maybe I'll just throw whatever in my suitcase and steal from yours. Just imagine it now, Mina, us strolling down Fifth Avenue wearing matching chic pantsuits..."

"Sounds like some real 'badass boss' stuff."

She squealed again and thanked me at least a dozen times until I managed to get off the phone.

The smile stayed on my face as I left the bathroom and went back to my seat. My fingers flew across the screen, and in ten minutes, Trinity had a flight booked, changed our hotel reservations, and sent a car over to retrieve Eloise.

My travel companions definitely heard my conversation,

but no one seemed to want to talk to me about it. They were all focused on their own phones, doing who knows what, while I fidgeted in my seat and received a barrage of texts from Isabella and Eloise.

After an hour, our conversations fizzled out, so I put on my headphones, turned on Eloise's "Fierce Women" playlist, and stared out the window.

These days, I was constantly surrounded by humans, vampires, witches, body guards, politicians, and business associates, but somehow, I felt lonelier than I ever had in my entire existence. How is it even possible that a person can be surrounded by so many people and still feel so alone?

Before Uncle Derrick's death, I had him and my parents. While the latter were mostly absent, it was at least comforting to have them flitter in and out of my life, and now, with all of them dead or gone, I was on my own.

Sure, I had Trinity, and as wonderful as she always was, I didn't really get a chance to sit down and chat with her regularly about nothing. Eloise would be a welcome addition to my queen errands, but I knew it was only temporary. Wyatt rarely spoke, and when Jax did, he was direct and to the point.

Theo had his witch family, Philip, and whatever other vampire friends I didn't know about. I wondered if he still kept in touch with Cara after we spent that night at the vampire club downtown a few months ago, but I hadn't asked about her since.

I pulled up our last conversation on my phone, the one before all the planning for this trip, trying to figure out why he ended it so abruptly. I wanted to talk to him about it and clear the air, but I didn't necessarily want to have the conversation here, with the pilot, crew, and the twins, so I texted him.

I think we need to talk.

Theo looked at me, expression unreadable. *About what?*

Our last text conversation was full of jokes and banter right up until the *Gazette* article came out and made things awkward between us, and I wasn't sure why. I was up front with him about why the unveiling was important to me, to all of us, and that was the end of our conversation. Nothing nefarious or dramatic, just radio silence.

Everything.

His eyebrow twitched, so I clarified. *I just feel like so much has happened these past few months and we haven't really gotten to talk it out, aside from our brief chats after the noble meetings. I was hoping to fill you in more on what's been happening with me and you could do the same.*

I didn't like putting myself in a vulnerable position, but if I didn't give him something, I was afraid we would stay stuck like this. I wanted to be comfortable around him again, playing chess and talking throughout the night, but he seemed disinterested.

Theo nodded at me, and I offered him a smile that went unreturned as the crew prepared us for landing.

12

Walking around New York was as different from London as I could have possibly imagined.

People were everywhere, simultaneously ignoring and hating everyone at the same time. It seemed as if everything blurred around us. The speed of movement and the sounds were incredible to take in while we all craned our necks to gaze up at skyscrapers and incredible architecture.

Jax and Wyatt were on edge, determined not to lose me in the crowd as we crossed the street, and Theo trailed along, taking in the scene.

The summer heat seemed to rise up from the concrete below my feet. Even though vampires handle the extreme weather far better than humans, I was relieved when we stepped in the vast air-conditioned lobby of an office building.

Trinity scheduled me for a photoshoot and quick interview before we were set to check into our hotel, timing it perfectly with Eloise's arrival. After that, I had a dinner planned with some district representatives and then a small break into the night until everything resumed in the morning.

We checked in on the first floor of the office building, only to be ushered up in a private elevator by a woman who introduced herself as Lucy.

"We're so glad you could fit this into your schedule," she said brightly, not at all intimidated to be in close quarters with four vampires.

She led us through the office, a modern-looking setup with cubicles and organized chaos. A few people gawked at us, and almost everyone had their phone out, documenting as we crossed into the area designated for the photoshoot.

"As I mentioned to your secretary, a number of designers provided outfits. Actually, that's an understatement because they all *begged* me to put you in their clothes. We have a few racks here for you."

Lucy opened a door to reveal a large closet packed to the brim with outfits. There was a small changing area set aside and a table with jewelry. The floor was nearly covered with shoes.

A few other women joined us, all gushing over my hair and jacket, both of which I spent no time on today, and ushered me inside.

"There are a few chairs over there if you want to wait for us to finish up," Lucy offered to the male vampires.

"I'll stay," Jax said, staying fixed in his position within a few feet of me, while Wyatt and Theo accepted her suggestion.

Lucy frowned. "Well, there's just not really a lot of privacy—"

"I'll stay," he repeated.

Lucy looked to me for help, but I smiled as if nothing was amiss. "Ready?" I asked her.

I wish Eloise could have been present for this portion of the trip. She would have loved playing dress-up and gushing over the eyeshadow colors and hairstyles, and Jax was a very poor substitute.

Lucy micromanaged every single look, ensuring I was comfortable with what they wanted to dress me in. I didn't put up too much of a fight on whatever they wanted to do, even indulging them by putting on a few different dresses. They were, however, dismayed that I would not be willing to remove the metal choker around my neck. I didn't mention that it wasn't by choice.

"Do you have your crown with you?" Lucy asked brightly.

"Unfortunately, no, it's at home for safekeeping," I told her.

She frowned but caught herself after a few beats. "Sorry," she said, dropping her voice to a whisper. "This is my first byline, and I want everything to be perfect."

"It's okay," I said. "Is there something else I can do for you?"

"No, no, you're perfect. Now that we have our favorite outfits picked out, we'll actually move ahead with the photo spread. You're going to be on the cover of our September issue." She said it like I should be very excited, so I tried my best to grin and match her enthusiasm.

"That's great," I said. "But nothing will come out sooner than that?"

"We hadn't planned on it," she admitted. "We wanted

to do a big photo spread with captions from you gushing about your favorite designers, looks, styles, whatever you want to talk about."

Internally I groaned.

Isabella should have been here in my place. She would have lived for this. I, however, was fairly useless with this sort of thing.

"Nothing vampire-related, then?" I asked.

"Well, of course you can talk about whatever you want, but I think our readers are interested in learning more about who you are, the human side of you," Lucy admitted. "Like, for example, who does your make-up?"

"Oh, um, I do it."

"What?" Lucy exclaimed.

Between taking photos against a backdrop, occasionally seated and with a fan blowing my hair out of my face, she asked me questions, and the photographer snapped candid behind-the-scenes shots.

Lucy seemed very impressed that I did such a symmetrical cat eye on myself, and even more so that I was self-taught through YouTube. We gushed over some of our favorite products and channels.

She peppered me with more questions, and I fit in some of my soundbites on equality for vampires, our work with the blood distribution network, and little stories about going to high school. She laughed hysterically when I asked her if she thought a graham cracker was a cookie or a cracker, surprised that I even was familiar enough with human food to question the categorization.

Wyatt, Jax, and Theo seemed to be bored enough to hold a conversation with one another. I was dying to know what they were talking about but too distracted to focus on their words. Plus, the rap music from a small speaker combined with my focus on answering Lucy's questions made eavesdropping challenging.

Finally, it was time for my last outfit and set of photographs.

"Oh, I think this is the cover look," the photographer cooed. "It's brilliant work."

One of the many magazine assistants spent the duration of the shoot off to the side with a box of costume jewelry and a headband, emerging at the end with a makeshift crown. She picked all silver pieces and a few chain-like strings of metal and arranged them beautifully in my hair.

"You should make more and sell these," I told her. "I'll be your first customer."

She blushed thoroughly, muttering her gratitude before finding the confidence to ask, "Do you mind if I take a picture of you wearing it? It really is amazing with the gown."

I glanced down and shifted uncomfortably. Compared to my normal look of pantsuits and jeans, this dress felt incredibly revealing. It was a sleeveless, floor-length gown with a high neck and made almost entirely of gemstones.

When I video called Isabella to make sure I wasn't making a tremendous mistake, her minute and a half of screaming helped quell my nervousness. My human emotional side was definitely rubbing off on her.

I tried to walk confidently in the sky-high heels in front of the camera. It was only a few steps, but I was grateful when Jax stepped forward, offering me his arm until I got into place.

"Cut the fan," the photographer said.

One hairstylist stepped up and smoothed my hair, which was pin straight for this shot.

The photographer passed off the camera to someone else as he approached me. "Okay, Queen Mina, for this one, we want ethereal. We want transcendence between human and vampire. We want fierceness and glamour. No posing, just be yourself, and I'll do the rest. Okay?"

"Sure," I said, even though it seemed like all of those things conflicted.

As they tweaked the lighting, I fidgeted in place.

I watched them all move in unison, making the slightest changes. Jax kept his gaze fixed on me and the people in my vicinity while Wyatt paced around the office, making those who weren't directly involved with the shoot a little uncomfortable, but as I looked around, I noticed nearly everyone had abandoned their computers in favor of staring at me.

Finally, the photographer indicated we were ready to go, and after fifteen minutes of holding the "perfect pose," I was finally finished.

The humans dispersed, and not wanting to risk falling in the heels, I balanced on one foot while undoing the buckle of the other. Theo, who stayed off to the side so far, stepped up.

I reached for his hand, but he knelt down, undoing the buckles quickly himself before he accepted my grasp. I smiled at him, and the flashes went off. I turned, confused, as the photographer shrugged.

"Just keep going," he encouraged, taking pictures as I lifted the edge of my gown and stepped out of my shoes.

I reluctantly dropped Theo's hand to follow Lucy and get out of the borrowed items. I was almost hesitant to give the crown and dress back, but it felt good to slide back into my own clothes.

"Thanks for everything, Lucy," I said as we shook hands. "Don't hesitate to reach out if you need anything else for the piece."

"You're an absolute gem, Queen Mina."

"Congrats again on your first byline. And thank you everyone else!" I turned to address everyone watching us. "I appreciate your work and can't wait to see everything when it's finished."

After the hours of questions and business of the shoot, I was all too content to sit in a quiet car as we idled in traffic on the way uptown to the hotel. Humans seemed to grumble about being delayed, but it gave me a chance to watch people and stare at all the stores and restaurants while sucking down blood from a bag, which was a necessity after the shoot.

Trinity texted me, confirming the location of my next meeting, and we went back and forth on the details and what I needed to expect.

Also, Eloise is all checked in and waiting for you. I've emailed a link with your room information and mobile key access.

I smiled at the thought of her being all alone in a gigantic suite in the middle of Manhattan, probably jumping on the bed or raiding the minibar, or whatever it is humans do. We were lucky that there was an opening on a flight so quickly, but I still wished she could have arrived earlier.

I should have taken pictures from the shoot because I

knew Eloise would freak out whenever they came out, but it was a shame we had to wait until September to see them.

Would it be totally inappropriate to ask the magazine to share some stills? I asked Trinity.

We have full approval over the photos, text, and quotes. We'll get everything in the next few weeks to give them enough time to make changes before publishing.

I didn't even know that was an option we had. *Got it. Thank you!*

When we finally made it to the penthouse suite of the hotel, I barely stepped inside before Eloise launched herself at me. Jax and Wyatt watched with curiosity as Theo accepted a hug as well before she started dancing around the room with excitement.

"What is this make-up you're wearing? I love it! It's *so* dramatic and *so* New York. I can't believe I'm here!"

Eloise then took it upon herself to show us around all the bedrooms, one of which she already claimed for herself. Seeing her so enthusiastic about something as simple as hotel-provided robes and slippers made me smile, and the stress I had about the next meeting melted away for the moment.

"And we have a freaking *butler* on call if we need anything. Too bad you vampires can't get blood on demand, but you bet your ass I'm getting waffles at ten o'clock tonight."

I laughed. "Whatever you want, Eloise. New York is yours."

It was a massive change from last fall when she refused to let me buy her a pair of tights without a hole in them, and I was happy to do it. Even if Eloise didn't win a scholarship on her own, I would have paid for her education and whatever else she needed.

In fact, once things were more stable with vampire-human relations, I planned to sit down and do a thorough review of the finances with Trinity to see what other things I could do for humans who needed help — but for now, I had to keep going with the current agenda.

I laid out all the clothes Trinity packed for me and hung up the ones that were slightly wrinkled in the travel process. I had just slipped on a pair of gray wide-leg cropped pants and a white sleeveless shirt when Eloise screamed from the living room.

We all rushed in, expecting her to be held at gunpoint or something, but she was crouched by the minibar with her phone in her hand.

"Look at this," she said, tilting the screen in my direction.

Eloise had shown me this celebrity gossip website before, but it was odd to see my own name on there with the headline: "VAMPIRE QUEEN MINA GETS COZY WITH MYSTERY MAN AT PHOTOSHOOT!"

Theo glanced over my shoulder. "Mystery man," he said, chuckling and shaking his head.

I snatched the phone from her hand and scrolled down. Sure enough, there were a few blurry photos from the end of the shoot.

Eloise commented on how fabulous my outfit was, going off about the designers I was draped in, but I focused on Theo's expression in the photo. I spent a fair amount of the shoot concerned he was bored out of his mind, but he looked far from it with his hand in mine.

I understood why the writer of the gossip article assumed there was something between us.

"Your majesty, the car is downstairs," Jax said.

"Where are you off to now?" Eloise asked.

"New York wants to be the first city to offer restaurants specifically for vampires, but everything is stuck in health department hell right now," I explained, choosing not to look at Theo as I spoke. "I'm meeting with some representatives and other officials over dinner to try to get things moving along. Are you two going to be okay here?"

"I'm sure we can find something to entertain ourselves with," Eloise said with a grin.

13

Photographers swarmed me at every possible opportunity.

I thought I'd gotten used to it in London, but the attention on me seemed to increase immensely after the pictures of Theo and me were front-page news.

Frankly, I didn't know what was so interesting about me getting out of vehicles, trailing behind Eloise as she walked into a store to grab something for lunch, or waiting for the okay from Jax and Wyatt to go into a building, but my movements — and Theo's — were heavily documented.

Everyone but me seemed to be ecstatic at the coverage.

The royals loved the positive attention. I was sure they were spurred on by the crisis communication company. I just wished I was tagged and mentioned in all the work I was doing for vampires, not gossip about who I was with or what I was wearing.

Even Eloise was getting contacted on social media by clothing companies asking if they could send her merchandise. As much as I could, I tried to pivot to my talking points and vampire rights and equality, but it all came to a head on the third day in New York.

They had converted our hotel suite into a studio of sorts. Trinity arranged for backdrops and lighting to be brought in so that news outlets could come in one right after another, maximizing the publicity and my time.

Jax and Wyatt were ever present and always lurking around, but Eloise and Theo flittered in and out throughout the day, coming back with armloads of stuff they bought while exploring the streets. Somewhere in between visiting Union Square and walking around Gramercy Park, Eloise and Theo struck up a genuine friendship and now had a slew of inside jokes to reference.

I was incredibly jealous, but I wasn't sure of which person or if it was the entire situation. I tried not to harbor any resentment, especially when Eloise dug into a bag of chocolates I left sitting on the minibar.

I refocused on the interviewer who just sat down behind the camera. Most interviews had been formal and business-like, but before this man even asked me a question, I recognized the logo from the gossip site that first published the photos of Theo and me.

"You have ten minutes," Jax grunted.

I wished Trinity had joined us in the city — she would have been a much more personable handler in comparison.

The interviewer straightened his tie, even though he wasn't on camera, before speaking. "So, you've been the talk of the city this week, Mina. Or should I call you Queen Mina? Your majesty?"

I smiled. "Mina's fine," I told him, even though he seemed to patronize me.

"Okay then, Mina. Tell me, what has life been like for you since vampires unveiled themselves?"

This was a question I had been asked a few times already, so it was easy enough to answer. I just had to skip over the fact that I was on a temporary pit stop in chasing down a three-hundred-year-old vampire.

"Honestly, my day-to-day has been largely the same, except for interviews like this," I explained, trying to relax and act human as I spoke, even though my routine was far different from most of theirs. "I run several businesses and am well connected with organizations and groups within my community, so I have a very full schedule of meetings and planning. I'm sure it's pretty boring compared to what most people think they know about vampirism from watching and reading."

He chuckled. "And from what I've been able to find, you have quite the legacy of vampires to follow. Specifically, your uncle, Derrick Byron."

"Yes, we were very close."

"And his death was very sudden?"

I frowned. "It was."

"And local papers reported it to be cancer," he said.

He stopped speaking, but there was an insinuation there.

I was specifically told to keep the details of his death as vague as possible — the last thing we needed was for everyone in the world to know about the hazard of dead blood.

"They did."

"So you're saying vampires can die of cancer? That there's no long or eternal life?"

"I believe it has been widely reported that vampires have an extended lifetime, not an everlasting one," I told him, my words coming off sharper than I intended. "But I'm no journalist, so perhaps you could double-check and get back to me."

"So how exactly did your uncle die?"

"Next question," Jax barked.

One of the many things I loved about humans was their tendency to be unpredictable, but this human had an undertone of smugness in his questions that irked me immensely. I held my own, but in this case, I didn't mind Jax using intimidation to push the interview forward.

"Your uncle was long known as one of the richest men in Pennsylvania."

"Is there a question in there?" I asked politely.

"It's interesting to me that your media coverage didn't exist until relatively recently. One would think it's a big story that someone so young would become the CEO of a number of organizations and inherit a nice sum of money."

That was because we actively worked to keep me out of the spotlight. We didn't need interviews about the teenage multimillionaire to deal with as we prepared for the unveiling.

I smiled. "If you would like me to discuss any of the businesses, I am more than happy to, but I'm not interested in discussing my personal finances."

"Fair enough," he said, giving me a once-over. "That's an interesting necklace."

I touched my neck. "Thank you."

"Where did you get it? I'm sure our readers would love to know where they can purchase one for themselves."

"A friend gave it to me."

"A friend? Would that friend be—" He looked down at his notes. "—Theodore Allard?"

My eyes flickered over to Theo, who sat beside Eloise on the couch. Both of them were watching me verbally spar with this interviewer.

"Yes," I said simply, not wanting to give him a nice juicy soundbite to use as clickbait.

"Are you two dating?"

I laughed. "I'm a businesswoman trying to encourage humans to accept vampires while fighting for the rights of us to be set up for success and integrated into society, but all you want to ask me about is my personal life?"

"It's definitely more interesting than your talking points on vampire identification," he deadpanned.

"I'm so glad you brought that up because I'd like to address that specifically." His expression was sour, but he let me talk. "You can quote me directly as to saying it's against our individual rights to be labeled as such. We all already have social security cards, driver's licenses, and, in many cases, passports. To force us to undergo another label is an expensive, fruitless endeavor. I'm sure we can find a better use of everyone's time and resources, and those vampires who have lived comfortably and anonymously for decades can continue doing so."

Once I finished, he shuffled the papers in his lap. "I have some screenshots of your social media channels that I was hoping we could take a look at together. You up for it?"

The crisis communication company would love it if I got airtime discussing the pictures from my sleepovers, Homecoming, and the other more humanizing activities I took part in.

"Of course."

I hoped for high school stills, but instead, I got a barrage of photoshopped pictures, notes of support, and a few marriage proposals. I laughed at the absurdity.

"So you can see why I am interested in more information on your dating life. Well, it's not just me. It seems everyone wants to know the truth. Are you or are you not dating Theodore Allard?"

"Time's up," Jax said gruffly.

He waited for the interviewer to leave on his own, but he wasn't moving fast enough for Jax's liking, so he grabbed his arm and practically shoved him and the cameraman out of the room.

I collapsed into the armchair next to Eloise and accepted a handful of chocolate candies. "That was exhausting," I admitted.

"I thought vampires didn't get tired?" Eloise teased.

"Anyone who says that has never had eight hours straight of journalists asking them questions."

"Theo, now that they know your name, do you think you'll get offers for free leggings, too?" Eloise asked him.

He rolled his eyes.

"I am sorry about that, Theo," I told him, but he waved me off.

"All part of the job," he said dismissively.

"What's next on the agenda?" Eloise asked brightly.

I checked the schedule that Trinity sent me. "Isabella should be at her home now if we want to get ready to head over there soon. Both of you are invited," I said to Eloise and Theo. "But I understand if you want to do something else."

"And miss meeting another queen?" Eloise balked. "You think I'm crazy enough to say no to that?"

Theo merely shrugged.

"Come on, let's go have solo girl time and get ready," Eloise said. "You boys better clean up, too."

I loved how my best friend, so human and feisty, ordered around three fully grown, powerful vampires. Before we could lock ourselves in the bedroom, Jax kindly reminded me that the windows were bolted shut this high up, so there was no use in trying to sneak out. I could break it if I wanted to — we both knew that — but I didn't plan on it.

Instead, we refreshed our make-up, did our hair, painted our nails, and talked.

Eloise was days away from finding out who she'd be rooming with in her dorm, and we talked through all the best-case and worst-case scenarios. "But what if she, like, is into weird stuff?"

"What kind of weird stuff?" I asked. "Drinking human blood?"

She giggled as she fixed a smudge of eyeliner under her eye with her knuckle. "What if she collects porcelain dolls or loves pictures of rodents and wants to hang them in our room?"

"Well, you could always live with me and commute down for class," I suggested lightly. "There's more than enough room at my place... what?"

Her expression was a mixture of surprise and flattery. "Did you just ask me to move in with you?"

I didn't do it intentionally, but in the split second I considered her answer, I wondered why I didn't do it sooner. Eloise turned eighteen months ago, and she was an adult capable of making her own decisions.

"If you want to," I said tentatively. "It would be nice to have you around, but I'm sure you want the true college experience. If you want to come back on the weekends or whatever, though, I'd love it."

She squealed and threw her arms around me.

"Careful of your nails," I warned, knowing she was awful at letting them dry long enough.

Her smile flattened when she pulled back. "There is something I've been trying to figure out how to tell you, and I have been waiting for the right opportunity to. And now's probably not it, I guess, but I kind of feel guilty keeping this from you, especially because you keep doing all of this stuff for me and—"

"What is it?" I asked.

She sighed. "Well, it's Charlie."

I frowned. "Is he okay?"

"Yes, he's more than okay." She paused, pursing her lips for a second. "He's kind of dating someone. I'm sorry to tell you this. I've been asking him to, but he reminded me that it has been a while since you two were kind of together and it'd be weird if he just messaged you out of the blue about it."

"Oh," was all I could offer.

"He met this girl a few months ago at orientation for school, and she's been pushing him for a relationship," she explained. "I think he was kind of hanging on to the idea that maybe you two would figure things out, but the longer it went on, the more it became obvious that wasn't the case, and you're not upset, are you?"

I considered it.

Back in December when Charlie and I faced each other with my property gate between us, part of me thought we'd be able to reconcile. That I would fall into the routine of being a vampire queen, he'd continue on living his human life, and maybe it would work out for us to be together someday.

But as time moved on, and the more I settled into reality, the thoughts of him gradually faded out. It wasn't malicious or purposeful, we just both started living separate lives, and I was perfectly fine with it.

I didn't want to put Charlie in harm's way or force his hand into becoming a vampire, which he would have had to do if it was known that a human was aware of our existence back then, and ultimately, I got what I wanted.

Charlie would live a very full and human life, and I was glad to be a part of it, even for a brief amount of time.

But my life would not be solely human or revolve around the complications of being with one. I could romanticize being with him, but in a practical sense, I had no desire to be. I was too focused on paving the way for other vampires to live life on their own terms, just like I always wanted to do. I smiled at the thought.

"I am the furthest thing from upset," I told Eloise.

She breathed a sigh of relief. "Okay good, now I can tell you about how awesome this girl is without feeling like a jerk while doing so."

14

"You look amazing," Eloise encouraged as I fiddled with the hemline of my dark blue dress. "Trinity has amazing taste. You should trust her choices more."

"It's a bit short." Even if it had a high neck and sleeves to compensate for it, I still felt a little uncomfortable with the skin on my legs so exposed.

She rolled her eyes. "Modesty is one of the most annoying things about vampires. I mean, what's the point of being a mysterious blood-drinking creature if you can't be a little risky with your outfits. Come on, Mina. You're not in a convent! You're a gorgeous young queen."

"Eloise," I scolded between my teeth, but she smiled devilishly.

During this exchange, Theo looked everywhere but at me.

We were all dressed up, more than usual, at Isabella's request. She lived for glamour almost as much as she lived for blood, and I warned Eloise about some of Isabella's more expensive habits, which only made her more excited to get going.

Miraculously, traffic was light as we coasted down toward the Village, where her three-story townhouse was located. She greeted us regally, and Eloise barely tore her eyes away from the extravagant crown on top of her head as she led us up the front stairs.

Isabella deposited Jax and Wyatt with her own security guard on the first floor by the indoor pool, then gave us an abbreviated tour of the house. It was beautiful and spacious by New York's standards. Eloise half-whispered an awed compliment in every single room, but when we got to Isabella's closet, Eloise couldn't hold it in any longer.

"Oh my gosh, look at this gown." Eloise clasped her hands together, as if she couldn't bear to touch anything. "Mina, you need to up your game. Look at these!"

Isabella laughed. "I've been telling Mina this for months. Her pantsuits are—"

"Chic but boring," Eloise finished. "And, no offense, Mina, I know your uncle had your crown made, and it's beautiful and everything, but Isabella's is such a *statement.*"

I looked at Theo, as if he would somehow take my side in this situation, but he shook his head, wanting no part of this discussion.

"Oh, you think this is one? Just wait a minute." Isabella opened one of the cabinets on the wall, revealing an entire lighted shelf setup and eight crowns.

Eloise legitimately gasped at the splendor.

"I warned you," I reminded her.

"You should see the collection I have at my actual house Upstate," Isabella beamed. "Would you like to wear one?"

Eloise opened and closed her mouth a few times. "I, uh, yes."

They spent five minutes figuring out which one would look best with Eloise's outfit, one of the green dresses that Trinity included for me, and then they had to find earrings to match. By the time we made it to the dining room, Eloise was completely decked out in jewels.

A human dressed in all white brought up a tray of food, some rice and steak dish from the smell of it, for Eloise and three wine glasses of blood for Theo, Isabella, and me.

"AB-negative," Isabella said, knowing it was my favorite.

"Theo's actually the one who got me into it," I told her.

"Oh really?"

"Why don't you tell her the story of our wild night out in Pittsburgh?" I suggested, trying to get him talking for the first time since we arrived.

Theo leveled with me and set down his glass. "I assume you've been to a blood club?" He directed the question to Isabella, who nodded.

Eloise set down her fork in exasperation. "Excuse me? There are vampire *clubs*? I'm going to need all the details of this. And possibly to go to one, like, right now."

Isabella laughed, and Theo filled her in, and she reacted appropriately horrified on some of the details.

"And you thought it would be a good idea to take Mina there?" Eloise asked in disbelief.

"I didn't expect Cara to take her up to the roof," Theo admitted. "But I was impressed by Mina's control."

"Control? Over what?" Eloise asked before taking a bite of steak.

Isabella seemed surprised I never shared how difficult it

was for me to be around humans in the beginning. "Herself, of course."

Eloise chewed, processing this. "Mina, it's more difficult for you to be around humans than other vampires?"

"She barely spent time with humans for eighteen years and then she was standing feet away from a human with an open vein..." Isabella had to take another drink from her glass at the thought.

"And I'm not as strong as they are," I admitted. "With cravings or brute force or even speed. It's because I'm half-human."

Eloise swallowed audibly. "Have you ever wanted my blood?"

Theo gave me a pointed look, wondering if I was going to come clean about the day in the library with Eloise. "I... yes."

She laughed, as if I just admitted something as harmless as having a crush on her. "When?"

"Do you remember the day in Independent Study when you got the splinter?"

"Vaguely. Was that the same day you gave me the chocolate bar?"

I nodded. "You ripped out the splinter, and a drop of blood ran down your finger. It took everything in me not to launch myself across the table. But I did break the chair a little bit, holding myself to it," I admitted. "Fresh air helped, so I ran to Health and mistakenly took Brooklyn's seat."

"And thus began the feud of her hating you."

"There is a human in existence who doesn't like you?" Isabella asked, genuinely surprised.

"Oh, Brooklyn hated Mina before she even met her, I think. A new girl in school who caught the eye of Charlie Schenley was no easy feat." Eloise continued on, unaware of Theo's frown. "It would probably just be easier if Charlie and I became vampires then."

"No," I nearly yelled. "Absolutely not."

The immediate silence that followed my outburst was palpable.

"I was kidding," Eloise finally said. "But what's wrong with becoming a vampire?"

I sighed. "Of course there's nothing wrong with becoming a vampire. Did you not listen to me do eight hours of interviews today about how wonderful it is?"

Eloise rolled her eyes.

"But it's a huge decision. I mean, don't you want kids? To grow old at a normal pace? To enjoy food? To sleep? To let your hair grow?"

Isabella cut in. "But it's her choice, Mina."

I played with the stem of my glass. "I know, but... it's just a lot to give up."

"So that's it then, Mina?" Theo's voice was unexpectedly venomous. "Humans over vampires, is it?"

To my surprise, Eloise came to my defense at his attitude. "Mina didn't ask for any of this. And I know you didn't either, Theo, but at least you had a chapter close on your human life and a new one open as a vampire. You've had plenty of time to adjust, but you're not cutting Mina any slack. She had, what, two months to explore her humanity and then was shoved into ruling an entire region of vampires, most of whom have been outright hostile to her?"

Eloise tossed her napkin on her plate, a show of being over this conversation. I got the feeling this was one of the things they discussed when I was tied up in meetings the past few days, and it was coming to a frustrating head in front of me.

"But you're sitting here, licking your wounds about Charlie when you don't even realize how lucky you are to be with someone who is as thoughtful, devoted, and beautiful as Mina? She's busy doing her queen stuff, okay, so just get the hell over yourself and support her and be with her the way she needs you to be now because she is crazy about you, and you're an idiot."

Theo's jaw ticked in irritation at her scolding.

I could only wonder if what she said was true, but I didn't get to ask questions before he stormed off.

"Finally, someone said it," Isabella murmured as I glared at her. "What? You've been dancing around him for months. Just get it over with already. Follow him."

She waved me off, and I listened, jumping on the opportunity to clear up any misconceptions between us.

I chased Theo up the stairs and was momentarily sidelined by how beautiful the view was before I saw him, leaning over the edge to look at the street below.

"Well, that was harsh," I said.

Theo looked at me, smiling tightly. "And not entirely wrong."

I shook my head. "Eloise doesn't understand everything that you've done for me."

Theo ran a hand through his hair, his way of not accepting my words.

"Oh, come on, don't give me that look. From the first

time we met, you've encouraged me to explore both parts of myself and have been my most loyal friend. Well, maybe aside from Eloise." I stopped talking and took a step toward him. "Theo, you've been there for me like no one else has."

I reached for his hand, but he shook me off.

"Don't do that, Mina," he begged.

"Don't do what?"

"Comfort me like you want something more, like you don't have a human boyfriend waiting for you back home—"

"I don't have a human boyfriend, Theo," I interrupted. "I thought you were teasing me by calling him that when he was at my house."

He stared me down. "Why would I tease you about something like that?"

"Why would you think I'm with him?"

"Because you didn't deny that this unveiling was for him. Because you were so adamant about him not becoming a vampire. Because you ran away from me, presumably back to him, after you kissed me." He broke off after that, mulling over his own words.

"Theo," I started. "I'm a queen. I don't have a ton of free time to get distracted by silly romances."

Those words offended him more than the ones Eloise said. "Silly romances?" he repeated.

"Just look at Uncle Derrick. He never—"

"King Derrick was a great king, but he was lonely and *sad*, Mina."

"How dare you?" I snapped, teetering between anger and hurt.

Theo's phone buzzed in his pocket, but he ignored it, keeping his eyes fixed on me.

"Who is it?" I asked, a relatively stupid question given that he hadn't pulled it out to check. "Is everything all right with the nobles?"

He laughed sardonically. "See? This is your problem, Mina, you're all business, treating me like a subordinate and nothing else."

The buzzing stopped and started back up again. I ran my tongue over my fangs, too irritated to even bother arguing with him again.

He angrily pulled it out and checked the screen. "The nobles want us back."

I closed my eyes. "We need to continue on to Europe after this."

"They're threatening a mutiny if you don't return immediately."

"Is nothing ever easy?" I asked rhetorically, pulling at the ends of my hair in frustration.

"Let's go prepare for the return." Theo moved away from me before I agreed.

"This conversation isn't over yet, Theo," I promised him.

"Yes, your majesty," he said back, setting the tone for the rest of our time together in New York.

15

"We don't care that the witches have put you on some crazy errand or that the other royals want you to run around all over Manhattan to do their bidding," Thomas said. "We have enough problems here, in our own region, to deal with at the moment."

He and Margaret still didn't shy away from sharing their opinions. I encouraged them to be vocal, as I did everyone, but that didn't mean the criticism was easy to take in.

The rest of the nobles shared his sentiment, and none of them seemed interested in my explanations or problem-solving. They just wanted to vent, so I let it happen.

Under the table, I checked a message from Isabella. *I meant to ask you in person, but obviously we got distracted. How are your parents doing?*

It was an odd question, considering they were in her region, not mine. *My mother calls occasionally, but we haven't spoken in a while. Why?*

Isabella took a minute to respond, which was a rarity

for her. *They didn't check in last month with my secretary. I'll have someone go and see what they're up to. Will report back.*

Some days it hadn't sunk in that I banished my parents from the region. They weren't overly helpful or emotionally available, even by vampire standards, when they were around, but I had to admit it would have been nice to have family nearby with Uncle Derrick's passing. I relied on Trinity to advise me, and the other royals, but I craved the sort of all-encompassing trust I had with my uncle. It was reassuring, to say the least, that there was someone else on the planet who only wanted the best for me.

In most situations, I tried to think of what he would do if he were here to guide me. I hoped he would be proud of the decisions I made, even as I forced my concentration back to another noble who was echoing Thomas's sentiments.

You've been more than accommodating. I heard Uncle Derrick's voice in my head. *Time to push this forward.*

"While you've been off gallivanting around Europe, we've been watching in horror—"

I immediately cut off the noble. "I think I've heard enough for now," I told him. "Let's focus on solutions or end this discussion."

"How do you propose we remedy this?" Theo asked from across the table.

His cool mask of indifference didn't faze me, as it was one I were accustomed to seeing the entire journey back to the mansion. He didn't even break as Eloise gushed about the marvels of flying private, telling me I'd officially ruined travel for her forever by spoiling her, and then attempted to pull the twins into conversation for an hour.

If Eloise felt comfortable enough around them to tease them publicly, I couldn't even imagine what she would do once she moved into my house.

And that was when the realization hit me.

We vampires were coming at this all wrong. We'd been fighting for equality without taking the step to merge our ways of life. We hoped we could continue to pressure the human governments to allow us to integrate while still, essentially, keeping the ruling law separate.

To truly be successful, we would have to do exactly what Eloise and I were doing — integrate into one place.

We would continue to have hiccups and challenges with keeping human and vampire dealings separate, creating arguments within our own communities instead of focusing on adapting to each other.

"I hear you all," I said. "The royals and I have been focusing on our national and global campaign, and aside from a few small interviews and errands, I haven't done enough to affect the change in our own region. As the Queen of Appalachia, my priority is our region, and I will do a better job of showing it. While I encourage you all to come with solid ideas the next time we meet, I'm taking the first step and forming an organization specifically to promote vampire and human relations."

"What will that entail?" Margaret asked.

I had to think quickly on my feet. "First, we'll begin by getting a small group of humans and vampires together, and we'll copy the press-hungry playbook that the royals have been using nationwide. We'll show them how well we're integrating in our own community and work to change the ongoing perspective in the wider region."

"I would like to participate," Margaret said. "If possible."

"Of course," I said. "Any others?"

No one volunteered.

After the nobles dispersed, Theo with them, breaking our tradition of debriefing, Trinity and I brainstormed a shortlist of people we could get involved with.

By the end of the week, we had an agreement from a local celebrity, a city council member, and of course, Eloise. It was a small but mighty group, and by all accounts, successful. After holding a press conference announcing the formation of the organization, we started to do regular human activities together.

Every passing day left the witches and other lives in danger in Europe, so I moved as quickly as I could.

We went back to the Indian restaurant Charlie took me to. Thankfully, the photographer didn't capture Margaret's look of disgust at the human food, but he caught her smiling once. The city council member was incredibly diplomatic, asking Margaret and me plenty of logistical questions, and we discussed more opportunities to get involved with the community. I saw dollar signs in his eyes when I offered to sponsor a few fundraising events in conjunction with the hospital.

On a mercilessly warm day, we went to a Pirates game. We sat right behind home plate, maximizing our exposure as best we could. The local celebrity, the daughter of some university trustee who started a clothing line, put up a ton of pictures of us on social media that gained thousands of comments and reshares.

By the time we took a trip to Kennywood, people recognized us enough to take more paparazzi-style photographs of us. It was like being in New York all over again, only with rollercoasters and carnival games. I used my vampire coordination to knock over a stacked set of cups with a ball and win a stuffed parrot for Eloise, which she put in her newly claimed bedroom in my house.

The crisis communication company seemed off-put because I did all this work without notifying them, but apparently, their polling was so overwhelmingly positive that they encouraged the other royals to copy my approach once again.

"So what's next?" Philip asked me at the next noble gathering, a week after the last.

Philip had been absent at the last few meetings because of his work with the blood distribution network, but I assumed Theo kept him up to date.

"We have one more event planned and then I will have to dedicate more of my time to the other duties from the royals and pick back up on my request from the witches." Before any of the vampires could vocalize their hesitation, I added, "Margaret is now formally in charge of the organization, so moving forward you will get updates from her on the project."

I nodded to her to stand and address the room.

She stood proudly, addressing the others. "We're going to be tackling city by city, so next I will work to select a group in Cleveland and then..."

Delegation was not my strong suit, but I tried. There was only one of me, but with so many smart and capable vampires and humans in the region, I needed to trust and assign more responsibility to others. I was already comfortable enough with this in the human companies, but honestly, it was because they were already well-established and successful when I stepped in. Now, I requested updates, advised, and encouraged others to bring their expertise.

It shouldn't be that difficult to replicate in this setting, but tensions and stakes were incredibly high at this point that I had trouble letting go.

As I continued to listen to Margaret, the strangest sensation rolled over my skin.

It was so slight at first that I ignored it, thinking that my body was somehow reacting to stress in some sort of phantom pain, but it became too persistent to ignore. It felt like an electric current was circulating through me, trying to find a place to escape.

Theo's eyes met mine, his expression transforming into the same devastating one I saw on Isabella's roof.

Just as I was about to mouth "You, too?" to him, the metal around my neck warmed.

His gaze dropped to the choker, which had tightened. It was a slow movement, but I reached up with my fingertips, feeling that it was, in fact, shrinking. My skin, impenetrable to needles, fire, and other normal objects, ached as the metal dug in.

This talisman was supposed to be an object of protection — not strangulation.

Thinking on his feet, Theo pretended to get an urgent message. "Margaret, I'm sorry to interrupt you, but Mina, I believe there's an emergency with Isabella you need to attend to."

I stood up, and everyone else did, out of respect before they bowed.

"My apologies," was all I sputtered before I sprinted out of the room.

It would have been faster to drive to Eva's, but I didn't think I could properly hold a steering wheel while I clawed at the metal digging into my skin.

My legs moved the fastest they ever had in my life, and it still took me nearly ten excruciating minutes to arrive at the apothecary shop.

Despite it being midday, the closed sign was turned, and instead of dealing with the doorknob, I sprinted straight through it, sending shards of glass everywhere.

I collapsed to my knees in the courtyard as my entire body convulsed.

The pain in my neck was unreal. My body reacted the same way it did when I needed blood or was threatened, but whatever was happening wouldn't let it come to fruition. My body rebelled internally, but it was excruciating.

"I figured that would get your attention," Eva said simply.

The flat line of her mouth indicated that she didn't necessarily enjoy doing this to me.

The pressure on my neck eased slightly enough for me to look up at her. She snapped her fingers, and the force of relief on my neck at the metal going back to its normal position made me fall forward.

I caught myself on my palms and inhaled a few breaths to right myself.

"Get up, Mina," Eva demanded.

I slowly stood up, touching the indentation at my neck.

"You're going to be just fine," she reassured me. "You'll be back to normal soon enough."

Residual tremors coursed through my body. The pain of my gums holding my fangs in against my nature seemed like nothing compared to what I just endured.

"You could have just called if you wanted to talk," I said hoarsely.

"I have called. And texted. And emailed. Your secretary kept putting me off, telling me you're preoccupied with vampire matters."

"And you didn't trust Theo's updates that we would restart the process soon?"

At that, she paused. "My nephew hasn't spoken to me since you had us over to your lovely home."

That was news to me. "So this was a cruel way to get both our attention?" I surmised.

She shrugged. "My familial locator spell put him at your home, but I assumed he would join you here."

"You interrupted a meeting with the vampire nobility," I snapped. "He stayed behind to keep the peace."

I don't know why I felt like I owed her any explanation. This woman had put me in danger and now physically harmed me, all in the name of doing her bidding, but somehow through it all, I actually felt bad for her. My family was dead or exiled, but to be so close in proximity and be cut off had to be a level of awfulness I couldn't comprehend.

"Theo and I are planning to fly out on Monday," I told her. "I just had a few things to wrap up before we went."

She nodded, giving me a few breaths to regain my

composure and stand up. "You don't like me, I get it," she sighed. "But there's something you need to see."

I put my hands on my hips, still feeling a little shaky. "I don't have a problem with you, Eva," I said truthfully. "Unless you're sending me off to slaughter or trying to choke me with a necklace you forced on me."

Instead of responding, she handed over a stack of papers.

At first, I brushed them off, thinking they were just a collection of photos of Theo and me from New York, from the photoshoot and on the street. But then I saw the messages below them.

I flipped through the pages. Each one got more detailed and threatening the longer I looked.

"Who?" I asked, handing the stack back to her after reading a particularly gruesome promise about how both of us would be torn from limb to limb.

"The vampire," Eva said. "I get dozens of letters each day. The threats are getting worse, and I'm gravely concerned if he joins you."

I understood her concern, but my patience was wearing thin. Being pulled in so many directions was grating enough, but I, too, didn't want to put Theo in any danger.

"Do you have an alternative in mind?" I asked her.

"There is no alternative," Theo called from the doorway.

His chest heaved in anger as he took in my still-shaken demeanor.

Theo crossed the room to stand between Eva and me, a protective move shielding me from her. He reached his arm back, and I grasped it, grateful that he'd put our differences aside to offer me this one small kindness.

The side he just chose surprised me, but Eva appeared devastated by it. "Theo, I just am worried about you and wanted—"

"To put your one minor concern over the safety of others," Theo interrupted. "I know you mean well, Eva, but could you imagine if the other vampires knew the truth about why their queen needed to run out so quickly?"

She pursed her lips, looking shameful for the first time.

"Or if something went wrong with the spell and you brought lasting harm? The witches in this region, hell, this country, would be rounded up so fast. Not to mention it's *Mina.*"

I squeezed his forearm, understanding the emotion he put behind my name. We were strained at the moment, but there were layers of feelings in those two syllables.

"The Evaline who raised me is neither cruel nor careless," Theo said. "And I hope to get reacquainted with her when this is all over."

Theo pulled me against him and used his vampire strength and speed to take me back home before either of us could say anything else.

16

I asked Trinity to clear my schedule. It was the first time in my reign I had requested this, and she seemed momentarily shocked by my request. Then it morphed into pride.

She watched me amble toward my bedroom before murmuring, "Derrick would be so proud of you, Mina."

I stopped, glancing at her over my shoulder.

"You don't have to give everything to be a good queen," she said. "It's just as important to take care of yourself as everyone else."

I nodded, then set off to draw myself a bath. It was the most relaxing thing I could think to do with this reprieve, and I stared blankly at the wall until the scalding water was high enough to sink into. I kicked off my clothing and slid in, uncaring that some water sloshed over the edge when I submerged myself completely.

It was the first time in months that I felt truly weightless.

I expelled all the air from my lungs and sunk to the

bottom of the expansive tub, which was big enough for me to stretch and flutter my arms and legs. It was difficult to succumb to the muted nothingness of the water. My eyes were closed, and the sound in my ears muffled the sounds of everything but the movement of my limbs. I couldn't hear Trinity, the twins, Eloise, or anything else outside the inches of water.

The deprivation of my senses helped me focus on the emotions I kept inside my chest all this time. The grief of losing Uncle Derrick. The guilt I felt on behalf of my father's actions. The nostalgia for my high school days of classroom learning and teenage drama. The pressure I put on myself to succeed.

These emotions stayed buried deep inside, just like the loneliness I didn't attempt to overcome in my day-to-day life.

I carried it all alone, keeping everyone at a distance. This was my job, as the Queen of Appalachia, to use my power, influence, and actions to create a better way of life for those I was responsible for — it was the burden of wearing the crown.

Theo was right that I treated him, and everyone else, like subordinates. I thought it was unfair to unload the vampire problems of the region, the human problems of business, and my emotions on anyone else, but to Trinity's point, to be a good leader, a good queen, I had to take care of myself.

I told myself again and again that once we got through the first quarter, or through the planning of the unveiling, or the damage, I would give myself a break. But there would always be *something* if we continued on like this. A piece of legislation, an unhappy group of people, a problem that needed solving.

I couldn't make excuses anymore. I couldn't delay the inevitable by letting everything snowball into this mess inside my mind.

And today, essentially being dragged to a little apothecary shop by my neck, was my breaking point.

I stayed down in the water for nearly an hour, trying to revel in the buoyancy and work through the problems in my mind. With each solution, I allowed myself to resurface a little, and by the time I needed to take another breath, I felt as light outside of the water as I did in it.

Eventually, I gasped for a breath, and still dripping, I reached for my phone. I fired off emails to nobles, royals, politicians, and CEOs. I delegated tasks, canceled meetings, and freed up my own time. Trinity could have done it for me, but I needed to be my own undoing, cleaning up the mess and setting a new precedent moving forward.

I toweled myself off and smiled, feeling completely in control of my life for a rare moment.

There were still a few things and interviews I absolutely needed to handle myself, but my schedule seemed relatively clear until I was due to fly out on Monday with Theo.

Theo.

He carried me the entire way back from Eva's earlier in complete silence, not bothering to say goodbye before heading to his car, off to spend the rest of the evening doing who knows what.

I picked up my phone and shamelessly shot off a text to Trinity. *Does Theo have any meetings or events on the calendar tonight?*

No. Although Theo and Philip have a meeting tomorrow morning at eight o'clock with some representatives from Toronto.

Thank you. Please tell Jax and Wyatt to take the rest of the night off.

Will do.

I considered Theo an essential and important part of my life. Since I'd met him, he'd grown from a distrusted stranger to the person who stuck by me in so many pivotal moments, and the realization that I hadn't been there like that for him gutted me.

But I wanted to be.

I should have been open and honest with him from the moment I broke our kiss in the rainstorm. I'd kept him at arm's length, letting conversations falter and assumptions fester.

I couldn't fault him for his frustration toward me, but even then, he protected my reputation with the nobles and showed up, choosing to stand up for my safety over his life-long relationship with Eva.

It was time to live up to the pedestal he put me on and prove that I deserved him.

"Your majesty?" Jax called, intercepting me as I opened the door to my Jeep. "Can I take you somewhere?"

I swallowed the groan in my throat. "No, thank you, Jax," I returned, hopping up to the driver's side.

Before I could close the door, he wedged himself in to stop me from blocking him out. "I really must insist that—"

"That you listen to your queen," I said sharply.

"Yes, but—"

"No," I cut in again, holding my ground as fiercely as I

could muster. It was terrible timing for me to test the boundaries with him, given that the marks the necklace left were still fading, but I refused to back down. "I do not need your service this evening, Jax."

His ultra-rigid exterior faltered. "I must—"

"There will be no repercussions," I promised him, assuming that was his reason for hesitation. "The other royals aren't keeping tabs on our exact locations."

He shifted his weight, but he didn't loosen his grasp on the side of the door. "That's not it, your majesty."

I sighed. "Jax, please let go."

He hesitated, struggling with his next words. "Do you know why I wanted this job?" he asked quietly.

That one question stopped my movement and inner pleading.

Trinity vetted and hired Jax and Wyatt, but I never dug deeper into the root of their interest in this role. I'm sure there were far more glamorous things for vampires to do than follow around a teenage queen.

I'd been wondering about his and Wyatt's backstories for a while, but instead of asking the question to Trinity or one of the royals who might know, I just let my imagination flourish. If anything, it showed how desperate I was for amusement.

"No, I don't know," I admitted.

He was surely using this revelation to stop me from running off on my own, but I was curious enough to hear him out.

"My wife," he said before closing his eyes, like it was painful to say those two words. "My wife was murdered."

I frowned. "I'm sorry."

"By a vampire," he clarified.

That I did not expect.

"It was almost a decade ago, but it still feels like it was yesterday. My wife had a… rough upbringing. I understood she had past demons but didn't quite understand exactly what the details were at the time. I loved her with everything I had and would have done anything to make her happy, so I never pressed for details on her strange scars. I thought the fact that she went from one under-the-table job to the next, and felt a constant need to move, was endearing, not cause for concern."

He paused, eyes narrowing at the memory.

"I slipped up, putting her social security number on an application for a new apartment. It was right after we got engaged, and she agreed to stay in a place long enough to buy things like furniture and decorations as long as I signed the lease for us. I came home one night after a long day of work at the gym to find her completely drained and a vampire completely drunk off blood. We fought, and instead of offering me the kindness of death, he turned me. I was so wrought with grief that I couldn't even fight the process. In fact, I welcomed the pain."

I reached out, placing my hand on his thick forearm. It was a human gesture of comfort, one he looked at with a furrowed brow, but I felt compelled to do it.

He reached a hand up and squeezed mine before releasing it. "This is exactly why you need protecting," he continued. "You're half-human, your majesty, and you're able to see things that other vampires cannot. The changes you have made, and are making, are not only going to help vampires but humans, too."

I offered him a small smile. "I know."

"And by human laws, there is no statute of limitations on murder," he pressed.

I was absolutely aware of that information.

He dropped my gaze. "I hope to one day have the laws in place that will recognize these crimes, and all crimes vampires have committed, to be dealt with accordingly, and you're the one who can make it happen."

"And I will," I promised him.

"To do so, you need to remain unharmed. And that is why—"

"You've made your point, Jax," I said.

He held out his hand, gesturing for me to slip out of the driver's seat, but I shook my head.

"I'm driving," I told him. "You can ride shotgun."

Jax pressed his lips together, hiding a smile before we set off.

The silence that settled between Jax and me on the drive over to Theo's wasn't uncomfortable. Over these past few months, we'd spent a lot of time together, and it would be nearly impossible to fill all those hours with chatter. Then again, his confession over his wife's death and his hidden motivation was the most I'd ever heard him speak.

It was like we uncovered an additional layer between us, edging toward some sort of friendship or camaraderie, and I couldn't help but test the boundaries a little bit.

"I am curious, though," I started. "Most vampires I know don't retain emotions or memories from their human lives, but you've carried this with you and even dedicated yourself to the cause?"

He considered my point. "I don't know what other

vampires recall, to be honest. Our human lives are not usually a topic of conversation, and that might be a part of it."

"That vampires are too preoccupied with their new lives that they just let go of the old one?"

"Or they don't have a reason to hold on to their humanity like you and I do."

"Yes, I suppose not," I agreed.

I sped us through downtown, riding the curves of the highway a little more aggressively than I should have. Eventually, we crossed one of the city's many bridges, dropping us in an area not too far from Eloise's childhood house, and I tried to get a feel for the neighborhood at each stoplight. It seemed like a bustling area for twenty-something humans, with lots of bars, restaurants, and brand-name stores — the perfect place for Philip and Theo, two bachelors, to settle in.

I pulled to a stop in front of a six-story apartment building, thankful that there was an open spot and I didn't have to parallel park.

"I suppose I can't convince you to wait in the car?" I asked Jax.

He glanced at the building, then back at me with a raised eyebrow. "It's not part of my job to pry, your majesty, but can I assume you're here to visit with Philip or Theo?"

The question itself didn't surprise me, but the familiarity he had with this spot did. "You've been here before?" I asked.

"A few of us meet for poker on Sundays if our schedules align."

"Oh." Interesting.

"It's a secure building, and they're on the top floor, so as long as you don't intend to sneak out the bathroom again without your phone, I am happy to wait here and offer you privacy."

I smiled and jumped out of the car. "Thanks, Jax."

17

"So much for a secure building," I mumbled, sneaking in the main entrance as a human resident was leaving.

I didn't bother waiting for the elevator, instead using my adrenaline and vampire speed to jump up the stairs four at a time until I reached their front door.

Philip opened it before I knocked. "Your majesty," he said kindly, offering a slight bow.

"Hello, Philip."

He gestured for me to enter. "How may I be of service?"

Their apartment was the pinnacle of what I learned to expect from vampires — minimal decor, all functional furniture, and floor-to-ceiling windows overlooking the street below.

"Is Theo here?" I asked out of sheer politeness, already picking up on the mixture of metal, lavender, and sage down the hall.

He nodded and pointed at the door on the opposite end of the apartment. "Jax downstairs by any chance?"

"Waiting in the car out front."

"I'll go keep him company," Philip said, bowing once more before stepping out and closing the door behind him.

I was grateful that these vampires were so willing to oblige my want for privacy to talk to Theo, and part of me wondered if they all thought a discussion between Theo and me was long overdue. Having just learned about the event five minutes ago, I was unaware of the level of friend-liness that they shared, and I wondered if I was ever a topic of conversation in that regard.

Theo was undoubtedly aware of my presence, but he waited for me to knock before he spoke up.

"Come in," he called, and I smoothed the front of my dress, then opened the door.

There was something oddly intimate about being in someone's bedroom.

I came to that conclusion when I stood in the organized chaos of Charlie's bedroom in his mom's house. He had years of his life contained in his room, with all the trophies, soccer gear, clothing, and books strewn about, and it felt like I was stepping into a deeper, more personal part of him.

The feeling crept up again as I took in Theo's space, although it was almost the complete opposite of Charlie's. In comparison, it was almost barren. The dark wood furni-ture, exposed brick wall, and open closet felt ultra-modern, and the only true personal touch in the room aside from his neatly organized clothing was the shelving unit containing hundreds of records.

Theo watched as I ran my fingers over the covers, which all seemed to be in various stages of coming apart.

"Did you come to ask my opinions on early twentieth century jazz?" Theo asked.

I smiled and shook my head, turning to face him.

He still wore the slacks and button-down from earlier, but he discarded the jacket and rolled up the sleeves.

I enjoyed seeing him just a little undone. It reminded me of the first time we met in the backyard of my parents' house when I noticed he loosened his tie and unbuttoned the shirt at his neck out of habit, not comfort. One of the many things I liked about Theo was that he seemed to still do little things like that instead of clinging to the vampire norms to fit in.

"Are you sure?" Theo asked, crossing the room. "Because the progression of tempo from the 1930s to the 1940s totally changed the way music was listened and danced to, and you should know it."

"Why is it that all vampires listen to this particular genre of music?" I asked him, including myself in that grouping.

My parents were regular jazz radio listeners, and I found the voices and instruments to be incredibly soothing, like I was tuning into a different time of human existence.

"I can't speak for the entire population of us, but I think it's kind of peaceful and beautiful, and it reminds me of my parents."

"Your parents?" I asked.

I'd never brought up the topic, but I knew his parents died when he was a child. He was placed in Eva's care shortly after that, and she essentially raised him from that point on, which is what made the fact that he defended me — chose me — in this conflict even more difficult.

"I grew up in New Orleans, where jazz is practically a lullaby every single night, no matter what part of town you're in. After the car accident, the only thing I wanted from the house I grew up in were a few photos and these records."

I eyed the collection with a deeper appreciation now. "She's one of my favorites," I admitted, tapping my fingers on a relatively new record sleeve of Billie Holiday's greatest hits.

In a swift movement, Theo cued it up on his modern player, setting the tone for our conversation with Billie's smooth and slow voice.

He turned to me with a devilish gleam in his eye.

"What?" I asked, watching him approach me with obvious intention.

"Dance with me?"

He held out his hand, willing me to accept it, but I laughed it off.

"The first and last time I danced, it didn't end so well," I told him. Seeing his confused expression, I added, "With Cara, at the club."

"That was *not* dancing," Theo insisted, pushing his hand toward mine again.

"I didn't come by to dance with you, Theo," I told him.

"Then why did you come?"

"To talk."

"So talk," he said. "And dance."

I sighed and reluctantly accepted his hand.

We moved together slowly and cautiously in the pose appropriate for the time of the music. He had one hand on my waist, and I had one on his shoulder, while our others joined and swayed beside us to the music. His room wasn't exactly spacious, but we made use of all the available floor, twirling around on the hardwood.

As Billie Holiday's crooning wore on, I relaxed.

"This is nice," I admitted. "But it's not why I'm here."

He squeezed my waist gently, pulling me closer to him. "I know, but I'm enjoying it, anyway."

I smiled up at him. "How did we go from arguing in New York to a noble meeting to me getting choked out by your aunt via a necklace to dancing in your room?"

"I wouldn't say we *argued* in New York," Theo said lightly. "I think we were just trying to be honest with each other."

I stepped back out of his arms, breaking the romantic cloud we moved around in. "I don't think I've been honest enough with you, actually."

"Then try me." He wasn't impatient, necessarily, but I figured he was curious what I was doing here, standing in the middle of his room unannounced but still welcome.

I paused, giving myself a moment to work out exactly what I wanted to say. "I think you were right about me treating you like a subordinate, but it wasn't intentional. I haven't deliberately been pushing you away; I've just been so focused on what I need to do as a queen that everything else that was a priority kind of got pushed back."

"Like 'silly romances,' I'm assuming?" Theo asked.

I bit back a smile. "Do you remember when I told you I misjudged you?"

He nodded, no doubt recalling the words I said to him while we hid in the walk-in freezer in my house.

"Well, now I have something else to atone for," I admitted, dropping my gaze to his hands.

"Which is?" he said, the seriousness in his tone forcing me to meet his eyes once again.

"I don't think I've done you justice, Theodore Allard. Because you are not a silly romance."

It was I who misread his intentions in the beginning, who pushed him away after my uncle's death, and didn't fully explain what I felt for him, leading him to draw his own conclusions based on half-truths. It was time I made myself clear.

"But, Theo, I didn't ask you to choose between your family and me."

"I'm aware, Mina."

"I don't want you to put yourself in danger or to sacrifice your happiness because it's what you think I need."

He stayed silent for a minute. "So what *exactly* are you asking me for, Mina?"

"You're the one who has seen me from the beginning, who has supported me even without my asking, who has challenged me and encouraged me when I didn't even really deserve it. You're the one for me, Theo." I paused for emphasis, watching him hold in any sort of reaction. "And I was just wondering if you'd want me to be the one for you, too."

The smile spread slowly across his face, completely transforming him.

"I don't want to be your queen, Theo. I want to be your equal. I want to absolutely destroy you in chess; to explore the world of vampires, humans, and witches; to drink blood on rooftops and eat chocolate in Paris; to go kill an ancient vampire whose mission it is to terrorize your family." I put both of my hands on his chest and met his eyes. "If you'll have—"

Theo cut off my words with a kiss, unable to hold back his response for another second.

His mouth moved quickly, deepening the kiss by swiping his tongue along my bottom lip. The rhythm between us was better than any song I'd ever heard, and the movement of our mouths together was my new favorite dance.

His hands roamed along my sides, somehow electrifying every inch of me he touched. It was the feeling between us that caused the reaction in me, but the magic swirling beneath his skin added another, more exquisite layer to it. I slipped my fingers through the buttons of his shirt, needing to feel the bareness and his power with my fingertips.

Nothing in my existence had ever felt as right as being this vulnerable and open with him in this moment.

He broke apart to trail kisses along my cheek, then dropped to my neck, like he was trying to kiss away the earlier pain from the metal talisman.

"Theo," I whispered, but he was unfettered.

I gently pushed his chin upward with my fingertips in an attempt to capture his lips once again.

"Mina," he said, pulling back to look at me with a serious expression on his face. "I would really, really like to take you out. On an actual date like we're just regular people, two equals in a normal relationship."

"But we're leaving on Monday," I reminded him.

He dropped a kiss on my forehead. "Then we must settle for a first date in Madrid or wherever else you want to go in Europe while we chase after a mysterious vampire who can and probably wants to kill us both."

I laughed. "It sounds perfect."

18

Theo's hand felt heavy in my own as we walked through the Strip District, and Jax and Wyatt trailed along, taking up their positions in silence.

Margaret, working with Eloise's suggestions, arranged for us to have the next human-vampire outing here, starting with a tour of a small art studio, taking a group painting lesson, then a walk around before we sat down so the humans could eat lunch. Of course, a photographer would follow along, capturing flattering and humanizing shots of us all, which would circulate to local papers and any other website that wanted to publish them.

At first, Eloise's jaw dropped open as Theo and I approached the group, but then she took in our joined hands with a massive grin. Before she could squeal and cause a scene, I shot her a look not to react in front of the others.

It's not that the attention would embarrass me, but I wanted the focus to stay on the relationship building between vampires and humans, not spurring another round of publicized speculation on my personal life.

"Do you have room for one more?" Theo asked Margaret, who bowed her head to me and waved us inside.

I was actually looking forward to today — and for the opportunity to have a little creative time. I hadn't taken on an art project since the Homecoming parade float, which I never even got to see in person.

After a quick tour to look at the various paintings around the space, we all sat at a long table with various brushes and paint pots, along with a blank canvas on a tabletop easel.

Theo sat beside me, arm slung around the back of my chair, and Eloise stared at me with wide eyes from across the table. As a precautionary measure, she pressed her lips closed so firmly that they practically ceased to exist. I doubted she'd be able to remain quiet for long; her budding friendship with Margaret meant that they both kept up a relatively constant stream of chatter.

The studio worker walked us through the painting basics of how to best hold a brush and which ones are suitable for the specific movements one is trying to capture, then propped up a simple painting of flowers in a vase for us to mimic on our own canvases.

We spent the better part of an hour trying to recreate the painting on our own, and overall, the act of spending time together and talking was worth seeing everyone's awful renditions of the painting.

Theo took a monochromatic approach, smearing globs of blue paint on the canvas, while the others tried to stay true to the artist's actual color palette. My own attempt was rushed and sloppy, but Eloise insisted we hang them all in the house somewhere once they dried.

Then we went for a walk outside, stopping in front of different store fronts to check out the various items — and of course, get photographed doing so. A few onlookers watched us with interest, and I waved, realizing that they likely recognized me from all the other press coverage. Some people returned the gesture, while several others realized their staring and turned away abruptly.

The local celebrity in our group insisted we eat lunch at Primanti Brothers, and I was all too happy to order and try their famous sandwiches that had french fries and coleslaw stuffed between the two pieces of bread, along with the other ingredients. Theo and Margaret watched in mostly disgusted interest as the rest of us indulged.

"So, Mina," the city council member asked. "I wanted to let you know that in our next meeting, we're going to be discussing changing the nomenclature in some of our documentation, rules, and regulations to make it more inclusive of vampires."

"Oh, that's fantastic," I said enthusiastically. "I would love to send a representative to the meeting to listen in. Margaret, do you think Thomas would be available to join? This is a great next step for us."

As Margaret asked for details, my attention was pulled two tables over, where a middle-aged man sat with who I assumed to be his daughter, no more than thirteen years old. He was listening to our conversation and making snide comments while she sat across from him, trying to focus on her food and not his words.

Eloise caught my frown and followed my eye line just in

time for the man to say, "What do they think they're going to do next? Demand that dogs and cats have the same rights as us? You've got to be kidding me."

"Eloise, you don't have to—"

"How dare you!" she snapped loudly enough to earn the attention of everyone within a twenty-foot proximity.

"Excuse me?" His mock outrage was grating. "I'm just having a conversation with my daughter here."

"No, you're making her uncomfortable with your pathetic opinions."

"This is America, and I'm entitled to my freedom of speech," he retorted proudly.

"Yes, you're entitled to speak and reveal yourself as a total moron, just like I'm well within my rights to tell you that you're an ignorant slob. Vampires are beings who deserve the same rights and protections as any other living people who are able to contribute far more to the human race than you and your idiocy, so keep your bigoted comments to yourself or get educated and over yourself."

I was pretty satisfied that a few people whooped and clapped after her spiel, but for diplomacy's sake, I had to speak up.

"Thank you, Eloise, for your candor that I, myself, could not offer." I turned my gaze to the terribly embarrassed teenage girl sitting across from him. "I'm sorry that I can't offer you any help in this situation other than to encourage you to let no man make you feel less than you're worth, even if it's your own father. I had a father who spewed nonsense, and I didn't let that stop me from following what I knew to be right. You don't have to, either."

She nodded before she averted her gaze.

"Time to get the check?" Theo asked, squeezing my thigh under the table.

Eloise plastered a smile on her face as we parted ways with the others, but once we were in the confines of Theo's car, she went on an angry tangent for a solid ten minutes.

Theo offered a few nods and murmurs of agreement, but I pulled out my phone, checking a text I got from Isabella.

I sent my secretary to check in on your parents. The house was empty. And they haven't checked in for a few weeks. Let me know if you hear from them.

I frowned. *Will do.*

Another thing to add to my growing list of concerns.

"Okay, I think I'm done ranting," Eloise said, smoothing her hair back off her face. "And I'm ready to hear if there's anything new that you would like to tell me about."

Her tone was too smug for someone who just screeched every possible synonym for "stupid" from the backseat.

"Theo and I are together," I told her proudly.

It felt fantastic to say out loud and I'm guessing just as good to hear because Theo reached over and squeezed my hand when I said the words.

"Finally," Eloise breathed, earning a glare from me. "Oh, come on. It was *so* long overdue."

"You're not wrong," Theo admitted.

He suppressed a smile as he accelerated us on the highway and checked the rear-view mirror to make sure we didn't lose Jax and Wyatt, who were following in the car behind us.

"What are you going to do about getting older?" Eloise asked.

I turned in my seat to face her. "What do you mean?"

"Well, don't you still age? Since you're half-human? And Theo doesn't. Because he's a full vampire. You're going to look pretty funny..." Eloise trailed off, seeing whatever expression was on my face.

I hadn't considered that.

Being half-human, half-vampire, I expected to have a slightly prolonged life, but I couldn't be totally sure if I would age normally now that I'd fully matured. Currently, I looked my age and possibly would continue to slowly grow old, but Theo, changed at nineteen, would stay that way for the rest of his existence.

Not that vanity was my primary concern with everything else going on, but it'd probably look strange for a nineteen-year-old to be holding hands with an old woman someday.

"Hey," Theo said lightly. "I couldn't care less."

I frowned. "It won't bother you that I age when you stay the same?"

Theo shook his head and muttered to himself.

Slowly, the words turned into the chanting I associated with spellwork. I'd never touched him while he did this before, and I could feel the magic that buzzed in his skin change. It was moving through him, like blood in his veins, to flow out of his fingertips.

"What the hell is happening?" Eloise asked, gripping the back of my headrest in shock.

I blinked, and the nineteen-year-old Theo transformed into a different version of himself. He glanced sideways, offering me a glimpse at graying hair at his temples and the slight signs of wrinkles around his eyes.

He still looked handsome, of course, but just older, more weathered — more human, less vampire.

"No way," Eloise said in disbelief. "You're, like, forty now. Is that a vampire trick? You can alter your appearance at will?"

"When did you learn to do this?" I asked.

Theo answered my question first. "When you made fun of my haircut last year—"

"I did no such thing," I insisted.

"Well, when you reminded me that I'd be stuck with this haircut for my entire life, it got me curious about spells to alter my appearance."

"Okay, wait now, back up," Eloise sputtered. "*Spells?*"

Theo smiled and began filling Eloise in on the details of his family. I'd heard or pieced together most of the information before, especially now that I had the context with the London witches.

"I can't believe you didn't tell me there are *witches*," Eloise said accusingly to me once he finished.

"Well, I'm still a full vampire," Theo chimed in. "Not like how Mina's half-human, half-vampire."

"And you kept your abilities after you became one?"

"Yes."

"Did it hurt?" Eloise asked. "When you turned?"

Theo grimaced. "It doesn't always have to be so excruciating. But the vampire who turned me... it was not an act done with care. I now know I was sought out and turned for revenge on my family, which explains why Philip found me in the street near his apartment, delirious and blood-crazed."

"I'm sorry you were hurt," I said, squeezing his hand in

reassurance. "The turning process doesn't sound enjoyable."

Theo shrugged. "I think I had it worse than most vampires."

"From what Mina has told me, it's essentially like a blood transfusion, right?" Eloise clarified. "You're drained by the vampire slowly and then you're fed blood back to replenish yourself, happening over and over again until your organs and everything else inside you is dead or changed."

"Not that our kind is totally delicate with this sort of thing normally, but if there's at least some connection or emotion in it, I'm sure it's better than what I went through," he answered.

Eloise frowned for a beat before her eyes gleamed with a renewed sense of purpose. "So now that everything with that is taken care of, let's talk about the next item on the agenda."

"There is an agenda for spending time in the car together?" I asked.

"Well, this is the first and last thing on it," she started, and her tone already revealed guilt that I would not like whatever she wanted.

"Let's hear it."

She smiled brightly, sitting up and clasping her hands together. "Okay, so, I was just wondering..." She trailed off.

"What?" I prompted.

"Will one of you turn me into a vampire?"

Vampires aren't easily taken by surprise, given our advanced hearing and perfect vision, but her words jolted

Theo and me into very different reactions — him laughing while I gasped.

"Eloise, what?" It was all I could say.

"I've been thinking a lot about it," Eloise said. "And I want to do it. I want to turn into a vampire, to be strong and powerful."

"That's incredibly naïve for someone who I know to be so brilliant," I countered. "You're already strong and powerful, Eloise. You don't need to be a vampire for that."

She rolled her eyes. "And you know me well enough to know that I'm not one to back down from a decision, one that I've considered for weeks, and I'm telling you, I want to become a vampire."

"Said another way, you want to *give up* your humanity," I pressed.

"You're saying that like it's a bad thing," Eloise shot back. "I don't want children or to grow old or all those other things you mentioned at Isabella's."

This conversation was too emotional. I put all of my well-practiced negotiation and intimidation skills to use because this conversation wasn't between me and a noble or a politician. It was with Eloise. My best friend. My favorite *human* in the world.

It wasn't that I was opposed to her becoming a vampire; it was that I just wanted her to be absolutely certain that this was what she wanted for her life.

"I just don't think you're ready, Eloise. I did you a disservice by coloring your view of vampirism. You've seen my house, how Isabella lives in New York, the lavishness, but you haven't seen the darker side, and in some cases, the reality of being a vampire."

Her nostrils flared. "You think I'm that superficial that I see a nice closet and want to become a vampire?"

"No, of course not," I insisted.

"Isn't this what you wanted, after all?" Eloise asked, visibly frustrated. "Why come out to humans and fight for equality if you truly believe that being human is better?"

"It's not that. It's just—" I stopped when her words truly sunk in.

I put humanity on a pedestal, something that always seemed just out of reach and that I would never get to fully experience. I was projecting my own shortcomings on her, and it wasn't fair. But that didn't mean I was entirely okay with it just yet.

"You've known the truth for such a short time. How can you be so certain this is what you want?"

"Don't you just *know* when something's right?" Eloise asked, eyeing me and Theo. "Even if you can't really vocalize it, it's a feeling deep inside of you that's just... everything."

I couldn't dispute her claims, but I was a little awed at her explanation.

"I'll do it," Theo said.

I took in the tentative excitement on Eloise's features and the hard line of Theo's jaw.

"You will?" Eloise questioned.

He nodded. "To Mina's point, I just ask that you give it some time. I will change you, if it's what you really want, in a year from now. Wait, before you run off and track down a vampire club, you have to understand that I just want to give you a chance to understand everything you're signing up for and at least let us sort out some regulations and everything else we have, making it as safe for you as we can."

Eloise sighed. "That's fair, I suppose."

Theo reached for my hand once again, his silent way of seeing if I agreed. He grasped my hand in his fingertips, and I reluctantly returned the gesture.

"We need to focus on killing a three-hundred-year-old vampire before we can turn you, okay?" Theo said.

"Okay."

In another life, if I touched down in Madrid on a private jet with three beautiful vampires, I would be in teenage girl heaven, but now, I couldn't deny the ominous feeling as we landed shakily on a small runway in the middle of Spain.

I expected some grand sign that the protection spell for the witches had broken now that Theo crossed the Atlantic Ocean, but there was nothing — no great spark or mist or anything other than reviewing the logistics of the next few days. Still, the roughness of our landing and the overcast sky seemed indicative of what was to come.

My trip to London was used as part public relations tour, part relationship building, part errand for the witches, but this one felt like some undercover mission.

We spent the week constantly on the move, not even bothering to unpack our bags, chasing down even the slightest whiff of blood or vampire. I didn't hold Theo to the promise of a romantic first date, given that we barely stopped long enough to take blood, let alone focus on our relationship. The ever-present Jax and Wyatt didn't exactly set the mood for us, either, but we had bigger things to focus on.

On our tenth day, after making our way through all the smaller cities and towns on the way to the coast, we made it to the southern edge of Spain. We'd gotten a tip from one of King Isaiah's connections in the royal family that there had been an unusual spike in the murder rate in the past month around Málaga. Human law enforcement was baffled, but we suspected exactly who was responsible for the deaths.

Once the sun set and the brutal heat of the day tapered off, we huddled at a small table on the rooftop of our hotel. Humans booked this hotel at a steep price for the view of the water, but for us, it was the wind carrying the fresh scent of salt from the sea that made it worth every single penny. After almost two weeks of constant sniffing and tracking, our senses needed a break.

Staring out at the sea that separated Spain from the coast of Morocco made me feel even more eager to close this chapter and move on with the next one.

Unfortunately, we were really no farther along than when we started. I remained hopeful, trying to be patient, but we were running out of ideas for trying to figure out a path forward on successfully tracking the vampire down.

"And you're sure there's not a locator spell that can be done?" Jax asked Theo.

He shook his head. "Maggie says that they'll do another on the next full moon to ensure we're still in the right general area, but I can't do anything on my own. I just wish we had something, anything, to make the spell more specific... a piece of his clothing, a detailed description, hell, it would be great to even know this guy's name."

I ran a finger on the metal choker, hoping that someday soon we'd get to use it and be rid of all this.

From what I'd learned of their particular branch of spellwork, it was a living, breathing *something* inside them that they called upon. Witches channel it through themselves to manipulate the elements or combine powers with other witches or use spells, kind of like recipes, to do things.

Theo's magic remained when he turned, but unlike Eva, who relied heavily on the precedents of the witches set before her, he felt his powers instinctively. But like all witches, the power was amplified in numbers, which is why once we found the vampire, Jax, Wyatt, and I would distract him long enough for the witches back home and in London to subdue him through the talisman, while Theo focused on driving the weapon through the center of the vampire's chest.

It wasn't the best plan, but it was the only one we had.

My determination stopped me from feeling fear, an emotion that should definitely be at the forefront of my mind at facing a three-hundred-year-old vampire who can *kill* vampires.

"Mina, is it possible to leverage the network of vampire royals in this?" Theo asked.

I considered it. "It is an option, but I consider it to be a last resort. We won't be able to get access to, or hack into, human police databases without offering them an explanation. At least, I would have some hesitation if I were asked to do so without context in Appalachia."

"Why don't we start with a social visit?" Wyatt suggested.

I raised an eyebrow at his suggestion and the sound of his voice, something I rarely heard at all. Jax was definitely the more talkative one between the two, but the bar was very low — until recently, the most common phrase out of his mouth was "your majesty."

"A social visit," I repeated.

"Tonight, the human royal palace is having a very publicized event, and all the vampires in the region are invited."

"How do you know this?" Jax asked him.

Wyatt gestured to a television behind the bar, with news coverage of what looked like a big red-carpet to-do. The people on the television spoke only in Spanish, and I tuned it out as best I could.

"You're bilingual?" I asked, impressed.

"I speak ten languages and a few dialects, your majesty," Wyatt said simply.

I held in my laugh. The man who rarely spoke understood everything, which wasn't the worst trait or sentiment. But had I known, I wouldn't have acted as sole translator this entire trip.

"So, you think we just show up, make friends, and sell a vague cover story as to our presence here and our need for governmental information?" Theo posed.

"No," I said, an idea forming as he spoke. "We need to make our presence known. We've been playing defense, and it's gotten us nowhere. How much longer are we going to keep this up? I didn't have any success with this in London, and it feels like, once again, we're just chasing dead ends. What's the point in hiding and chasing shadows when we could draw him out?"

The three vampires stared at me, totally unmoving, until Jax quietly said, "I don't like this idea, your majesty."

"You don't have to like it," I told him. "It just has to work. Look, now that we've broken the part of the spell that keeps him here, what's to say the vampire actually stays? How long until he realizes he can country hop and slaughter all the vampires in our region? We should jump on this now, while we're hopefully still in the same place."

Theo reached for my hand. "Are you sure?"

I nodded. "Are you in?"

The three of them nodded without hesitation.

We took off immediately to change our clothes and freshen up. Trinity, thankfully, packed an array of clothing for all of us. Had I done it myself, I would not have packed formal attire, opting for low-key jeans and shirts. She, as always, thought of everything, including calling in a favor from King Isaiah's secretary to work the magic to get us on the guest list for the event.

By the time we pulled up to Palacio Limonar, a sprawling estate not too far from our hotel, the event was bustling. Wyatt checked in with a woman holding a tablet who had the same no-nonsense demeanor as Trinity, and we were immediately ushered in.

"Ready?" Theo asked, holding out an arm for me.

A mix of humans and vampires meandered at the entrance, and photographers lined up on the sides of the aisle, taking pictures of guests as they walked. Every few steps, they would stop and pose for the cameras, and Theo and I mimicked their actions. Jax and Wyatt stayed just far enough away to ensure they weren't in every single photograph.

I felt like I was back in the magazine office in New York, but this time, I didn't have anyone to guide me on how to hold myself or change my facial expressions. A few flashes hit in our direction, but it wasn't until about halfway down the aisle that I heard my name being called.

"What are they saying?" Theo asked.

"They are spewing nonsense," I explained. "They're all asking questions based on the current headlines of my personal life. 'Teodoro' is you, in case you haven't picked up on that."

He smiled. "Oh."

The group in front of us started moving again. I stepped to follow, keeping the procession in motion, but Theo grabbed my wrist, spinning me backward into him.

"You want to make a big splash, don't you?" Theo whispered in my ear. "Really get attention?"

I nodded. "For once, I'm keen to put myself in the spotlight."

"And I'm happy to reap the benefits."

I barely processed his words before he pulled me into an earth-shattering kiss.

His mouth moved quickly on mine, and his hands wrapped around my body, pressing me flush against him. I melted into him completely, succumbing to the warmth of his mouth and the buzzing beneath his skin. I wrapped my arms around his neck, holding on to him in fear that I couldn't stand on my own two legs anymore, which would quickly become a problem given our public location and the fact that we were trying to face off with an ancient vampire.

We finally broke apart as the shouts and camera flashes increased.

I couldn't help but smile at the smug satisfaction on Theo's face, but it quickly faltered when he pressed a hand on my back and sent a jolt of electricity through his fingertips. On instinct, my fangs descended, and the crowd of people gasped and yelled — thankfully, it was in an exciting way, not a horrified one.

"The Queen of Appalachia has arrived," he said, planting a kiss on my neck before we walked inside.

Technically, I was one of several vampire queens who arrived at the event, but I was likely the only one who received a panicked phone call from their secretary regarding the massive uptick in publicity.

Wyatt stayed at the perimeter of the room, while Jax followed us around the event, speaking to Trinity on the phone quickly but in hushed tones to update her on who we were speaking to and what topics of conversation we covered. Trinity simultaneously updated King Isaiah's secretary, who was researching who could help us with the task at hand.

In the few other events like this I'd attended, I played my part as minimally as possible. My role as queen meant I would forever be the face of the region and a key part of vampire culture, even if I didn't exactly appreciate all the attention. This time, though, Theo and I made it a point to enjoy ourselves and be seen as much as we could.

Getting nudges from the secretaries back in the U.S. helped steer our conversations, but mostly, Theo and I danced and clinked our glasses of blood with as many people as we could.

I, apparently, danced with an estranged member of the human royal family, only to be rescued by a Spanish billionaire playboy. He was a little too handsy while he spun me around the dance floor, but the number of people I noticed taking our picture was a decent trade-off. When the song ended, he clung to me for another, but Theo interrupted and politely asked for his turn. I watched over Theo's shoulder as the playboy's girlfriend, clearly an heiress or a model, slapped him across the face.

"Having fun?" Theo asked.

I glanced up at him, offering my most genuine smile. "I think I preferred dancing in your room to this, but it's not that bad."

"But here we get to watch Wyatt avoid getting spoken to at all costs." He spun me around, allowing me to confirm with my own eyes that he and Jax both had a few women eyeing them up. "And be subjected to all kinds of unflattering photos that we can hang up in your office."

I laughed. "So this is what you imagined for our first date?"

"Showing you off? Yes. Everything else?" He paused, eyes roaming around us. "Not necessarily."

I squeezed him a little tighter, knowing that the glass dagger was tucked in his chest pocket.

"Let's take a break," Theo blurted, signaling to Wyatt that we were stepping off the floor. "I think we've earned one."

Theo led me across the dance floor and up a set of empty stairs. We stopped on the landing, giving ourselves the illusion of privacy but staying within eyeshot of Wyatt and Jax.

The oversized window we stood in front of overlooked the expansive yard, which had a number of tables and even more people — vampires and humans — milling around, making casual conversation and drinking either blood or alcohol. We both faced outward, watching the scene in front of us.

I couldn't think of a time in my existence when I was ever any of those people — enjoying something just for the sake of doing so. I always had some agenda for being somewhere or talking to someone.

I thought I understood the responsibility I was undertaking when Uncle Derrick named me his heir, but we both thought we'd have years together to guide me until his eventual death. Being thrust into the role was taxing enough, let alone taking on the responsibility of the unveiling in such a short time and chasing down the vampire.

"Do you think someday we'll be one of them?" I asked Theo, not taking my eyes off the group of people laughing and talking under the twinkle lights.

"We are them."

I shook my head. "We're just pretending to be, Theo, but we aren't, really."

At this, he slipped an arm around my waist and dropped a kiss on my shoulder. "You're doing what you have to do to make all of this possible, Mina. The rest will come with time."

I knew he was right.

I never wanted a crown or to be anything other than a normal teenager, but I wouldn't be able to live with myself if I turned my back on the long-term gain and betterment of all vampires just because I wanted to do simple things like go to a movie theater or walk around the streets of London.

Still, something about this night, being in such a beautiful place with something so heavily weighing down on us made me feel a little hollow.

I sighed, forcing the air and the dejection from my body, and turned to face Theo.

He held on to the look of seriousness, ready to have a serious conversation if I needed it, but the lightness in his eyes and curve of his lips made me want to do anything other than stay in this melancholia.

Surely we could take a brief reprieve for ourselves before we had to go back to vying for attention on the dance floor...

I traced the collar on his shirt, curious if I could silently signal my intentions of what I wanted right now.

I hoped all the other vampires at the event weren't focusing on Theo's and my conversation, and frankly, I wasn't in the mood to talk anymore. Running my thumb over his bottom lip caused Theo's eyes to flicker to my own mouth. His gaze caught mine once more before our lips met, and everything else faded away.

Our kiss in front of the cameras earlier, while good, was stilted and posed. This one was just for us.

Theo wound himself up in my messy updo, causing complete and welcome disarray, while I gripped his neck and shoulders, begging for more pressure, more feeling, more Theo. His tongue swiped against my bottom lip, and I couldn't help but sigh into his mouth, permitting his entrance and giving in to him.

We *definitely* needed more time like this when this was all over.

The sound and flash of a camera outside the window caught our attention, and we broke apart. The photographer down below showed no shame at being caught, simply shrugging his shoulders before snapping more pictures.

Theo and I both chuckled at his actions.

"Do you feel better now?" he asked, attempting to smooth out my ruined hair.

"I do," I admitted, holding on to his belt loops. "I'm suddenly feeling very energized."

"Who needs blood or rest when you have me?" Theo asked.

I laughed. "Not—"

My words were cut off by the sound of screams. Theo grabbed my hand, and we sprinted down the stairs to see what caused the commotion. I got instant flashbacks to my failed ritual, but instead of an explosion, the lights cut completely, leaving us in near-darkness.

Last fall, Uncle Derrick and I, along with the rest of the vampire community, left as quickly as possible, fleeing from any potential danger. And although it turned out to be a fluke, self-preservation was our priority. Now, Theo, Jax, Wyatt, and I moved in tandem, headed in the complete opposite direction as the rest of the partygoers, trying to find the source of what caused this.

It wasn't as worrisome as an entire wall exploding, but it was out of character enough for an event like this to raise our suspicions.

The thought of successfully provoking a three-hundred-year-old vampire should have been terrifying, but the thought of our plan working exhilarated me enough to overtake that emotion. We tore through the kitchens, into the basement where the electric and boiler room was housed, and throughout the rest of the rooms in the space, but nothing seemed out of the ordinary other than the lack of people.

Strangely enough, there was a distinct scent of nothing permeating the space — not nothing, I supposed, but the absence of anything human or vampire, which was abnormal. All creatures left the signatures of their scents, but this void ran through the entire space. The more I thought about it, the more it unnerved me.

"Do you guys smell that?" I asked.

Wyatt offered me the closest thing to emotion I'd ever seen on his face. "The antithesis of existence permeates."

I didn't put it into those words in my mind, but it made sense.

A fresh round of screams rose outside, and the four of us sprinted at our inhuman paces through the main doors as the lights flipped back on. Illuminated on the side of the old, exquisite Palacio Limonar was a message, written in blood:

DEATH SEES YOU

20

We stayed around the southern coast of Spain for a few days after the event, waiting to see if the threat would surface again, but eventually, the royals — and even Eva — coaxed us to come back.

"It'll be safer if you return here," Eva pleaded after Theo finally relented to answering one of her many phone calls.

He looked at me while he spoke to her. "And possibly lure the vampire back to Appalachia?"

"If the vampire is aware of your presence enough to make a statement like that, then he might have already crossed over. We'll be stronger with you here, Theo."

The royals were happy with the public display I made and the press that went along with it — and one of the numerous companies we hired suppressed the bloody end of the evening from the U.S. news outlets.

Eloise and Isabella kept sending pictures back and forth in our newly formed group text, scouring the internet for every single image published of Theo and me. There were, apparently, fan groups on social media who manipulated our faces into popular movies and television shows and wrote fan fiction about our "love story."

It made me wildly uncomfortable, but Theo found it to be pretty entertaining.

We finally made it back to the mansion, and I sighed in happiness. As much as I wanted to explore and enjoy the world, it was nice to be home, cocooned in my normal surroundings and the memories of Uncle Derrick.

Jax and Wyatt unloaded the bags as Theo and I made our way to the industrial freezer for blood bags, but we stopped short when I inhaled upon stepping over the threshold.

Theo inhaled deeply. "Is that—"

"Trinity?" I yelled.

"In here," she replied, but I detected a slight undercurrent of shakiness.

We sprinted up to her office, and seated in front of her desk, as rigid as I remembered, was my mother.

"Mina," she whispered, standing up to offer me an exaggerated bow.

It had been months since I'd seen her or spoken to her, but she looked the same as always, frozen in time at the point my father turned her.

When I was younger, I used to sneak out of the house to watch humans interact, and one of the most fascinating relationships was between mothers and daughter. I grew up with the rigidness of vampires and minimal affection, but human mothers let their children drool and cry all over them.

At first, I found it repulsive how easily humans showed

their emotions and bodily fluids, but the more I studied it, the more I found it to be sort of endearing. It seemed to be another layer of love I never experienced, rooted in tenderness and adoration.

If Charlie's, Eloise's, or even Theo's parental figure showed up after months of being away, I imagined there would be smiles and hugs, but all I felt for my mother was emptiness and maybe a little pity.

After everything that happened with my father, she still stood by his side, choosing to exile herself with him instead of staying with me. I tried as hard as I could not to be gutted by that decision — her choosing a murderer and abuser over her own daughter.

I hoped I could someday do justice to those girls he harmed — but I made peace with the fact that my wounds, although not physical, would never heal, just like those victims would never recover.

"It's good to see you, Mina," my mother said, breaking what I realized was an incredibly uncomfortable silent standoff between us.

"Is it?" I asked, inhaling noticeably. I didn't pick up any trace of my father's scent on her.

She bowed her head, not out of respect for me but out of shame.

"Your mother has information for us," Trinity said evenly. "Perhaps we should all sit and discuss."

I shook my head, cutting off her pleasantries. "What information?"

My mother slowly raised her eyes to look into mine. "I have information on the vampire," she said so lightly that it was slightly unnerving.

"How?" Theo asked quickly.

"Your father," my mother started before collecting her words. "Your father has been in contact with his associates over the years. I didn't necessarily understand who he was interacting with… Derrick had him on so many projects."

My mother used a similar excuse regarding my father last fall. I knew she was out of the loop, but at this point, I didn't buy her pleas of ignorance.

Then again, it likely took courage or something like it to bring herself here, but I also considered the genuine possibility that it was a trap.

"Go on," I pushed, needing to pull as many details from her as I could.

"Isabella's secretary was very clear in her instructions of how we had to conduct ourselves in her region, and mostly, we were left alone. Back in March, I guess news about the upcoming unveiling had spread to most vampire communities around the world, and well, I'm sorry to tell you this, but not everyone is happy about it."

I stopped myself from rolling my eyes at her ignorance that I was unaware of the world around me, instead choosing to cross my arms on my chest, a very human gesture of impatience, and she began speaking quickly.

"The ancient vampire likes the status quo, but there was nothing he could do to derail the plans in motion, so he backed off."

"How did you come by this information?" Theo demanded, losing his composure more rapidly than me.

"I'll get to that, I promise," my mother said, looking at him uneasily. "But it wasn't until pictures of the two of you surfaced together… a descendant of the witch who overpowered him and the descendant of the vampire who helped her do it…"

"I'm sure that went over well," I said sourly.

"The day after your recent stunt in Spain, he showed up in person for the first time." At this, my mother visibly started shaking, a very un-vampire move. "His singular goal is to kill you both, and all of your relatives, Theo, and inflict as much harm as he can in the process."

I pressed my tongue against my fangs. "I will not let this happen."

"You don't understand, Mina," my mother pleaded. "He is unlike anything I have ever seen before. I know you think your father and I have shunned humanity completely, but this vampire… there's no trace of it left."

"I am not afraid of this vampire," Theo said, ignoring her words. "Tell me how we find him."

My mother blinked. "Mina, he and your father have found a similar sense of purpose in the moment."

"So they're together right now?" I asked.

She nodded.

"How did you get away, then?"

"They're quite busy with their planning and entertainment."

I refused to let my imagination go with that information.

"I ran all the way here," she admitted. "I left them last in Isabella's region, but they have been moving every few hours."

Trinity was in the process of alerting the other royals, and Theo busied himself on his phone with looping Eva and Maggie in on this news. But the sound of Eloise pulling up in my Jeep pulled my attention.

I listened to her quick footsteps, by human standards, and racing heart until she stood before me. "Mina," she cried, panic clear in her voice.

"What is it, Eloise?"

The tears ran down her face as she said, "Charlie's missing."

Eloise's words coupled with the way my mother averted her eyes threw me into a fit of anger I hadn't felt since the last time my father did something despicable. I shed all of my humanity, falling into my vampire instincts.

But unlike when I showed off for Eloise and Charlie months ago, I didn't maintain my control. The fearlessness overcame me. My muscles moved like a predator, and I pounced on my mother, pinning her to the ground in anger. I clawed at her while she held her hands up defensively.

It took Theo and Trinity both to pull me off her, but even with their additional strength, my ferocity fought back.

"Mina," Theo pleaded. "You have to calm down."

I hissed at him, kicking my legs out to break out of his hold.

"Hurting your mother is only going to hurt you," he said.

I didn't care.

My vision blurred, as if my body emitted so much raged heat that my eyes fogged up.

"Jax," I snapped.

He appeared by my side in two seconds.

"Go to the Schenley residence and call me to confirm the scent."

He nodded, sprinting off with speed on the mission and purpose that grounded me enough to completely regain my composure. Eloise's constant stream of talking and worrying held my attention until Eva arrived, flanked by the witches from the night she created the talisman.

After Jax confirmed he picked up on traces of my father's scent, we moved from Trinity's office to the library, needing room to activate the spell. Even after all this time and the work I'd been doing to help them, the witches still regarded me tentatively. At first, they were too afraid to touch anything in my home, but Eva ordered all of us to clear the room, creating a large space in the middle.

I never pried into their power or capabilities, and it did me a great disservice, putting me at a disadvantage with a choker around my neck that allowed Eva to control me. Now, I refused to stand idly by in their spellwork.

"What is this?" I asked. "I didn't think you needed this much room for a spell."

"You said they moved rapidly, yes?" Eva directed her question to my mother, who stood beside a somewhat nervous Eloise.

"Yes, every few hours," my mother answered.

"This spell is not just a broad locator spell that is chan-neled by a full moon or a simple one that can track my kin," Eva explained. "Instead of a location, I will see flashes, which are obviously useless when the vampire is running around Europe, but now that he's here, it's possible that I'll be able to recognize his exact location and keep him there."

Theo regarded her with intensity, like there was something about her he hadn't fully started to trust again.

It was hard to blame him, considering the last time we saw her, it was after she choked me into submission.

"Let me see the spell," he said.

She balked. "You don't trust me?"

He didn't answer her question, holding out an expectant hand for her to pass him the book. The curious part of me wanted to flip through the pages, myself, but I watched Theo assess the words on the page quickly before nodding and passing it back.

"Satisfied?" Eva asked, attempting to sound sharp to cover up the underlying hurt in her voice.

"You have enough barberry for this?"

I recognized the name as the herb that Theo retrieved for her last fall while we were in the Strip District together.

She nodded. "Yes."

"And it's fresh?" Theo asked.

"I used a stasis spell."

"Good."

"Are you going to ask me a question about every single thing I do?" Eva challenged.

Theo's jaw clenched, seconds away from exposing his fangs, which would make everything worse.

"It would make me feel more at ease if you, at the very least, walked me through it as you're putting it together," I jumped in. "You'll recall last time I was left with this—" I gestured to the silver choker. "—and no explanation."

Eva sighed and started pulling items out of her bag. "It would be better if we waited until nightfall," she said. "Or until the next full moon."

"We don't have time for this," Theo snapped, stepping forward to help her pull candles, herbs, and all of her other supplies out.

With the witches busy lighting candles, mixing herbs and vials of liquid, I didn't get the outright explanation I was hoping for. But I couldn't help but watch their movements in fascination, how meticulous they were about the placement of each object in the circle until they joined hands and began chanting.

Theo rejoined us on the sidelines, standing between a skeptical Wyatt and me.

"How are we going to get a location out of this?" Eloise asked quietly.

"The most powerful witch, in this case Eva, will see a vision of it," Theo answered, explaining why his aunt stood in the middle of the circle.

When the chanting began, I expected a swirling sensation or something deeper, but the frustration in the circle was surprising. They chanted more viciously, squeezing their eyes closed. It was like a car that wouldn't start — no matter how many times you turned the key, it sputtered and refused to ignite.

"Theo," Eva gasped, extending a hand out to him.

He glared and refused to reach out to her.

"Put our differences aside, Theo. I know you're angry at me, but I need you. We need you. Mina needs you. An innocent human boy who got mixed up in all of this needs you to embrace your power."

The witches released one another to let him in the circle, backing up Eva's words. His gaze flickered to all of their resolute faces, and finally, he relented and took Eva's place.

Theo closed his eyes, and when the chanting began again, the light of the candles intensified. Eloise recoiled from the brightness, shielding her eyes, and yelped when everything began to move. She grabbed my arm instinctively, as if she needed to hold on to something to make sure what she was seeing was real.

The herbs, salt, and liquids swirled like the tornado Theo created on Uncle Derrick's gravesite. Instead of whipping around, they formed shapes, letters in a language I didn't understand. The shades of each witch's magic expelled from their palms, coming together to meet Theo's, a beautiful shade of electric blue, in the center.

He closed his eyes and surrendered to the whirlwind of their spellwork. It surrounded him, obscuring him from my vision and putting him in the eye of the storm. Watching him unleash his power, clearly stronger than the others' combined, proved he was just doing parlor tricks for me.

Being half-human, half-vampire meant I shared traits of both, but I didn't consider myself to have the benefits of either side. Theo, however, didn't have to be half of anything — he was a whole vampire with the benefit of magic running through him.

I stood frozen in awe at his movements, how effortlessly he controlled the spell with complete serenity. I wished I could go to him, to touch and feel his magic in this state, but I didn't dare move.

The movement stopped when Theo yelled and dropped to one knee, pressing his hand on the floor to steady himself.

The witches, too, stayed in their spots, hands grasped as

their words faded. They all looked exhausted from their effort, chests heaving, but it was all worth it when Theo opened his eyes to gaze directly at me.

"The warehouse."

"The... one with my father and the girls?" I asked.

He nodded solemnly. "Let's go."

Jax, having returned from the Schenley house, and Wyatt flanked me as we made to leave, but Theo remained blocked in the center of the circle.

"Eva," he growled.

"I do not want to put you in harm's way," Eva said. "Our original plan of Mina trapping the vampire and us helping out remotely still stands."

"When will you understand, Eva, that I'm no longer under the control of what you want?" Theo said harshly.

The witches held strong, trying to keep him trapped by refusing to drop the power interlaced in their fingers, but Theo shook his head before he flicked the air in front of him, sending a jolt directly into the chest of every single witch in the room.

They all dropped to the ground, and he stepped through easily to grab my hand and lead the way to meet a three-hundred-year-old vampire.

21

It should be like the movies.

We should be flanked by men decked out in protective gear, all whom have years of experience in de-escalating conflict, hostage retrieval, and taking down enemies. We should have a better plan than channeling magic through a piece of metal around my neck and a glass dagger. We should talk through every scenario, discussing contingency plans or anything at all.

But we don't.

"I understand if you want me to handle this on my own," I said to Jax and Wyatt, breaking the tense silence on the drive over. "I can't ask you both to put yourselves at risk—"

"Where you go, I go, your majesty," Jax said, interrupting and staring me down in the rear-view mirror.

Wyatt met my eyes, confirming that he felt the same way, and Theo squeezed my hand in reassurance while gripping the dagger in his other palm.

Us four vampires, distant witches, a metal necklace, and a dagger were our best hope for killing an ancient vampire and keeping a human teenager alive. I didn't know what kind of state he would be in or how far the vampire was willing to take this feud, but I couldn't let anything happen to sweet, human Charlie. I thought of Emma, so young and dependent on him. What if he didn't come home to her?

As we approached the warehouse, we didn't bother killing the lights or masking our presence. If he was as strong as he was rumored to be, he would sense us coming no matter what we did.

The same voided scent from the estate in Spain consumed us as we stepped out of the car, like we were stepping close to something that was so defiant of nature.

Theo shot off a text to the witches before his hand grasped mine resolutely, eyeing the choker for good measure.

The warehouse door swung open, and my father stepped out to meet us. He outright refused to meet any of our gazes, keeping his eyes firmly fixed at his feet. Even if he looked me directly in the eye, I doubted I'd be able to read whatever emotions or thoughts were swirling in his head — he was a vampire in all of his actions.

"Come," a powerful voice bellowed from inside.

I gasped at the sight of Charlie unconscious and tied up. I eyed the puncture wounds on his arm while listening to his ragged breathing and faint heartbeat. Charlie's scent had dissipated, like it was being smothered by the voided scent of this ancient vampire.

My fangs descended at the realization of what was happening.

The vampire started the turning process.

And I didn't know if we could stop it.

"I thought this would do the trick," the vampire said.

I laid eyes on him for the first time and gasped.

He must have been nearing eighty when he was turned. His hair was white and sparse, his skin peppered with dark patches and wrinkles. His appearance, overall, was feeble, but his eyes were crimson, venomous, inhuman.

He turned to my father. "The agreement is fulfilled. You and Marie are free to go."

My father left without bothering to acknowledge my existence. He traded me, his own daughter, and three other vampires for his own freedom. I seethed, renewing the promise to myself that if I got out of this alive, I would make sure he got what he deserved.

The vampire moved over to me so quickly I wasn't sure if his feet even touched the ground.

"Why don't we get properly acquainted? Queen Mina, is it?" He turned to look at Theo. "And Theodore, the promising young descendant of witches turned into a vampire at such a young age. And you two, I have no need for you now."

Trying to reason with this vampire might be the dumbest thing I had ever done, but I did it anyway. "If you will hand over the human, I will gladly send the others away."

"You value the life of this human that much?" The vampire was once again by Charlie's side, dragging a finger along the marks on his arm.

"I do," I said honestly. "I don't want him harmed."

The vampire eyed me before forcing his gaze over to Jax and Wyatt. "Fight," he ordered.

Jax and Wyatt, as if they were mere puppets, exchanged blows with each other. It was hard to watch both of them attack each other — even though no blood could be shed or true harm come to either by the other's hand — because they were not in control of their own bodies.

"Stop," I pleaded. "Please, stop this."

The metal on my neck tightened, contributing to my panic.

"Not yet," the vampire said, watching the fight with interest. "I want to see who wins."

Theo's fingers moved in spasms, and his mouth moved wordlessly as the blood encased in the dagger swirled.

Jax let out a grunt as Wyatt's foot slammed against his chest, sending him backward into the warehouse wall. The hulking blond vampire surged forward, continuing their sparring match and leaving a Wyatt-shaped dent in the plaster.

I hated myself for not doing more to stop it, but I feared I would somehow make the situation worse.

"Come here, Mina," the vampire said.

My mind fought against his words, but every inch of my body drove forward to obey his command. I tried to dig my feet into the floor, but it was like a string pulled me toward him until I crashed into him. He turned me, pulling my back against his chest so he and I could watch the scene together.

His icy fingers traced the skin on my arm. I tried to turn back to Theo, wanting to see how far along he was in whatever he was doing, but I couldn't move at all.

The vampire gripped my waist and shot us upward, hovering over the scene below.

"Theodore, while I am very interested to see what you intend to do with that piece of glass, I'd rather not deal with spilled vampire blood, even if it is quite old."

I couldn't turn to see exactly what happened, but the clang of glass on the floor — that thankfully didn't shatter — showed that Theo was also under the control of the vampire now. Charlie's heartbeat continued to fade as the fight between Jax and Wyatt increased. I thought I felt out of control in the past, but I'd never known a feeling like this before.

Rendered completely under someone else's control.

"What do you want?" I said through clenched teeth.

"Everything." The vampire soared higher, giving us both a full view of the scene below. "I'm the most powerful being in existence, but I've been trapped in shadows. My name is not known, and my mere existence has been called a myth among vampires. Now that you, dear Mina, have led the unveiling of our kind to vampires and assisted in lifting the curse, I will have my revenge. Then, I will have fame. Then, I will have power. And finally, I will have everything."

The talisman at my neck burned, firing to life. I recalled Eva's words when I first held the smooth metal in my hands. *"Not only does the spellwork carried within it rein-force the shield of your skin, but if you're in peril, we and others of our kind will use it to track you down. Once you find the vampire, we will funnel our spells through this talisman to subdue him, and you will be able to remove it and use it to your advantage, much like the metal chains that are in the basement of your home."*

I guessed this was what she considered being "in peril."

Whatever it was, I hoped it worked.

The metal on my neck melted down my body, back to its original liquid form, until it met the vampire's bare hands on my waist. When the heat met his skin, he threw me off him, and I crashed into Theo on the ground.

The vampire's full concentration in trying to remove the coiling metal from his body broke whatever influence he had over us.

"Take Charlie," I ordered Jax, who stood momentarily dumbfounded with Wyatt, both trying to regain their composure.

The red slits of the vampire's eyes rimmed with panic, and he fell to the ground, hissing and revealing the longest and sharpest fangs I'd ever seen. The rest of his teeth, yellowed and uneven, were sharp and stained with Charlie's blood.

With each second, the vampire transformed. It wasn't an outward shift, but I could *feel* the change.

It was that same vacant scent, only I pieced together exactly what filled my nostrils this time. It wasn't a vampire or human scent. It wasn't alive or dead. It wasn't any being; it was a lack of anything, defying the planes of existence, and he exuded it.

He fought the powers of the witches, glaring at me with a patronizing smile as he successfully stopped the momentum upward. This was a game to him, another event out of thousands in his life to pass the endless time. Wyatt sprinted in front of me, as if his body could shield from this horror in some way.

"Theo," I growled. "He's fighting it."

Since standing on his feet, Theo had focused his energy on preparing the dagger, but with my warning, he released a wave of electric blue mist from his fingertips, reinforcing the spell and rapidly mummifying the vampire.

"This isn't over," the vampire promised as the metal wound up his neck.

"For you, it is," I assured him.

Once the vampire was fully encased in metal, petrified in place, I allowed myself to collapse, sinking to the floor and feeling a weakness I hadn't experienced since I refused blood last fall.

Theo gripped the dagger between his fingertips, ignoring the growing restlessness of the boiling blood in the glass, fighting to be released.

Without hesitation, he took it and drove it into the vampire's chest. The glass finally shattered, and the blood seeped through the metal, burning everything in its wake.

The vampire remained held in place, and his red eyes stayed on mine as the spell overtook him, and his screams echoed in my ears long after he ceased to exist.

EPILOGUE
FIVE YEARS LATER

"There's still time to change your mind," Theo said, pulling back the curtains to take in the crowd.

I laughed. "What's one more little thing to handle as a queen?"

"Little thing?" Eloise shrieked, Isabella trailing in, ready to back her up. "There are thousands of people on your front lawn."

"Not to mention the millions of people on the live stream in twenty-six countries," Isabella added.

"Twenty-six?" I mocked. "That's it?"

Today was the fifth anniversary of July First, the day vampires unveiled themselves to humans.

The U.S. government refused to officially declare July First a national holiday, saying it came too close to the Independence Day celebrations. Each year, I worked with the local politicians to ensure that there were events happening in all states in my region, and as time passed, the celebrations grew bigger.

This year, the royals wanted me to hold the event in a massive venue or in the middle of a stadium, but I didn't want all the fanfare.

One would think after all this time together, they'd understand my distaste for the spotlight, but I had to coax them into letting me host it at home. Trinity and I set up a stage, media area, and space for the general public to gather on the lawn of the mansion. It was crowded in the street with all the human cars parked along it, but I wanted everyone to feel welcomed and invited, even if it put Jax and Wyatt on edge.

Thousands of witches, humans, and vampires celebrated together outside. From my vantage point, I couldn't tell who was who or what they were. I liked that feeling.

The first two years after the unveiling were the most tumultuous. We received every kind of pushback, fear, and rioting at making our existence known, and on top of that, I was caught up in the past mistakes of a witch and an ancient and powerful vampire. Of course, the wider population wasn't aware of the threat of the ancient vampire or that he was gone.

Even after erasing the threat, the relationship between vampires and witches in my region were still strained; although, Theo's relatives in London were very vocal and grateful for us. Yesterday, Maggie mentioned that they were starting discussions on their own coming out day, but with the tenuous history of witchcraft and persecution, it would take a while. For the moment, they were happy to support from the sidelines and learn from everything we continued to go through with humans, bureaucracy, and the court of public opinion.

"How much longer are you going to hide in here?" Eloise asked, using her vampire speed to jump to my side.

"This is *your* party, and you're already not in the center of it," Isabella said with a devious smile. "Shocking."

Over the years, the two of them had become thick as thieves, even more so when Eloise turned — holding Theo to his promise — and visited Isabella, eager for a taste of New York's vampire culture.

Now that she graduated, doing a sped-up five-year program to earn her bachelor's and MBA, she would help Theo and me found a new non-profit organization called The Center for Human and Vampire Relations. Margaret and our original group would also be a part of it, but we hoped to make an impact nationally, not just in our own region.

"You've had that crown for half a decade, Mina, and you're still not entirely comfortable wearing it," she said, smoothing her hair back so that Isabella's borrowed jewels shone in the setting sun.

"Not that it matters now, I suppose," I said, letting the smile spread on my face.

Theo pressed a kiss on my forehead, and I squeezed his hand reassuringly.

"Mina," Trinity said, standing in the doorway and clutching her ever-present tablet. "It's time."

I double-checked my appearance in the mirror, smoothing down the black gown I wore to my coronation before I followed her.

As I walked toward the stage, my eyes scanned over the attendees, landing on the roped off area where the media stood, snapping photos and taking videos to cover the celebration.

Charlie, on assignment as a junior reporter for the *Gazette*, smiled. He waved, making me feel as normal and human as he always did, and the glint of gold from his wedding ring caught in the light.

Even now, I felt guilt over what happened to him in the warehouse. I'd never forget the sight of him tied up and drained of blood at the hands of the three-hundred-year-old vampire. Thankfully, after receiving multiple blood transfusions and a cast for a broken arm, Charlie came out of it relatively unscathed. The only lasting consequence was anemia, but it didn't seem to bother him.

In his college years, he was an advocate for vampires, even creating a pro-vampire support group at his university. The group was small but very much appreciated, and it was actually where he met his now wife, who was just starting her career in local politics and running for city council.

I was very vocal in my support for her campaign, and I wasn't sure if it tarnished any journalist impartiality he had, but I always indulged his interview requests.

Every single day was a fight for equal rights for vampires, and we currently found ourselves at a crossroads.

Years ago, I recognized the challenges of navigating human bureaucracy, but as I began working with more progressive politicians, it became clear that trying to integrate wasn't the only issue — the biggest hurdle was having two separate entities creating laws for the citizens who lived there.

We'd been making important changes — updating

verbiage, passing new anti-discrimination laws, and working on a set of rules that somehow blended the human Constitution with the vampire Code of Conduct — but it wasn't enough.

To truly be equal, to work together, we could no longer operate as two separate entities.

I was the first to volunteer to give up my crown.

Of course, I would get to keep the beautiful piece of jewelry, but I would give up the title in hopes of a better, more equal life for everyone else.

Today wasn't just the annual celebration of July First; it was the abolition of the monarchy in Appalachia — or my "un-coronation," as Eloise called it.

I stepped on the stage to cued music, and the royals and nobles of the region recited a modified version of the same lines they recited at my coronation. The words, first written in the 1700s by the founders of the regions, focused on honor, duty, and responsibility, which seemed more applicable to me today than it did when the crown was first placed on my head.

After the ceremony and removal of the crown took place, I stood at the microphone and addressed the crowd, reaffirming the reasons behind the change and my hope for what we would accomplish moving forward. I spoke quickly, and the crowd hung on every single word.

I picked up on plenty of familiar faces as I spoke, but as I spoke the last words, I kept my gaze outward toward the clearing in the woods where Uncle Derrick's body lay in his grave.

"It has been a tremendous honor to be your first Queen of Appalachia, the first half-vampire, half-human to hold the title, but I am even more proud to be the last," I said with a tone of finality, earning a roar of applause from the audience.

A local rock band took my place on the stage, indicating the celebrations were now in full swing. Jax and Wyatt trailed behind me as I wandered through the crowd — a last request by the other royals was that I would keep them around as a precaution, and I obliged. With no immediate threat, they relaxed slightly. Instead of holding a six-foot perimeter, it was more like a twenty-foot perimeter.

"Can I steal you for a few minutes?" Theo asked quietly before placing a kiss on my knuckles.

I nodded, letting him lead me through the crowd of attendees, many of whom bowed and smiled when I walked past.

Jax and Wyatt trailed behind us, but I held out a hand, asking them to give us even more space as we took off alone, cutting through the woods for a minute to ourselves.

It was morbid that one of my favorite places on the property was where Uncle Derrick's grave stood, but aside from that, it had happier memories with him flying me into the night air — and of course, it was a special place for Theo and me.

"Do you remember the first time you took me out here?" I asked him.

He smiled. "Of course. I gave you a big declaration, you kissed me, and then you took off."

I rolled my eyes. "Not exactly how I remember it, but fine," I laughed, then forced my tone of seriousness. "It was such a pivotal moment for me, Theo. Your words 'Don't fight it' helped me in ways I don't think I can even begin to explain, but I think, finally, we're completely past it. Fighting the world around us, the labels we have, the problems that follow us wherever we go."

"I like to think that our most dramatic moments are behind us," he said, kissing me on the temple.

"I hope so," I admitted, staring at the grave marker beneath our feet.

"He'd be proud of you, you know. For everything."

I agreed with him wholeheartedly.

Uncle Derrick would be proud of me for every single decision and moment I'd lived without him, not just because I did it but because I did it while staying true to myself.

I'd managed to push vampires into human society faster than he suggested it would happen, and as of a month ago, enough legislation had passed to hold vampires accountable to human laws.

The FBI even allowed me to watch as they brought my father out in the witches' magically enhanced chains, which I handed over on the condition that they would turn a blind eye to where I acquired such an item. Eventually, they would get to discover the source.

My mother, while not complicit in his actions, would likely face charges. Any relationship I hoped we would build after she came to me all those years ago was ruined when she took off again with my father. It didn't take long for me to track them, or the witches to subdue them until I could turn them over to law enforcement.

When the news broke of his arrest, I came forward in agreement to pay one million dollars in restitution to each of the girls' families, and I eagerly awaited the details of the trial to be sorted out so I could testify against him.

His victims deserved justice, and so, in my opinion, did Uncle Derrick — but my father would never be tried for that crime.

"I talked to him," Theo whispered. "Derrick."

"What do you mean?"

"One of the last nights before he died. He asked me to come by while you were out running some sort of errand for him because he didn't want you to overhear." Theo paused, smiling. "You know he liked me the best."

I laughed. He had a strange fondness for Theo, even though I didn't trust him the first time I met him. He approached me in such a relaxed fashion that I took him for having ill intentions — I was so taken aback by someone addressing me that way that I questioned his motives.

But from the very beginning, Theo treated me as an equal, wanting to be by my side, and I was incredibly grateful that out of everything that happened, he and I stuck by each other.

"Derrick made me promise that I would be there for you, no matter what your role," Theo said, dropping down to one knee. "As my queen, my friend, my... wife. He used that word, not me. And it took us a little while to figure things out, but I know that no matter what happens, Mina, you're it for me. I want to spend the rest of my life with you if you'll have me."

He opened the ring box, unleashing a steady stream of rose petals that encircled both of us until my eyes fell on a silver ring with a ruby gem in the center.

"Will you do me this honor, Mina? Will you marry me?"

"Yes," I said without hesitation.

The ring slipped on my finger, and he pulled me into his arms.

When I first picked up the phone to call Uncle Derrick and argue over the details of me — the lonely half-human, half-vampire looking to find herself — going to high school, I was ignorant of the consequences and challenges that were ahead. But I was able to make my own world instead of finding myself in someone else's, and that's all I could have ever hoped for.

FREE GIFT FOR YOU!

Want to make your book an autographed copy? Head over to Jennifer's website and get a free bookplate!

https://www.jenniferannshore.com/bookplate

CONNECT WITH JENNIFER

Hi there,

I cannot thank you enough for reading my work. Truly, it means the world to me!

I'd love to connect with you on social media if you're up for it. I'm on all the major social channels, including TikTok (@jenniferannshore) and Instagram (@shorely).

And don't forget to subscribe to my email newsletter (jenniferannshore.com/newsletter) for bonus scenes, new release announcements, giveaways, and more.

All my love! —Jennifer

ACKNOWLEDGMENTS

"Metallic Red" and "Yes, Your Majesty" were a blast to write, and I hope you all have enjoyed my contribution to the genre with a modern day vampire coming-of-age romance series. I'm so grateful for your support.

To start, I need to thank my editor Taylor Starek, who encouraged and reassured me so many times throughout the process. Thank you for being just as invested in Mina's head as I have been.

Kelly Lipovich created another stunning cover for this book, and I'm in awe of her work.

Lindsay Hallowell is the reason why there aren't hundreds of extra "of" and "that" and "actually" words in this book — and I'm immensely grateful for her help with things like comma splices and consistency catches.

I need to thank all the beta readers (especially Emily Wright) and reviewers who shared so much excitement for Mina's story.

Of course, I can't forget Rachel Kilroy, for her endless loving friendship and beautiful photos to help promote my books.

Finally, to my friends, family, and husband, thank you times one million. If I become a vampire someday, I'll be sure to bring you all along with me for the ride.

ABOUT THE AUTHOR

Jennifer Ann Shore is an award-winning, bestselling author based in Seattle, Washington.

She writes romance stories that go a little deeper than the standard tropes. Her lineup of more than a dozen books includes standalones, a dystopian series, and a vampire series—with titles such as "Perfect Little Flaws," "Young at Midnight," and "Metallic Red."

Prior to publishing, she led an impressive career in New York, first as a journalist and then as a marketing executive, gaining recognition for her work from companies such as Hearst and SIIA.

Be sure to sign up for her newsletter on her website (https://www.jenniferannshore.com) and follow her on Twitter (@JenniferAShore), Instagram (@shorely), and TikTok (@jenniferannshore).

www.ingramcontent.com/pod-product-compliance
Lightning Source LLC
Chambersburg PA
CBHW071522110726
47908CB00003B/924